Cover design © 2018
Jana Heidersdorf, used under license

Edited by Lori Alden Holuta
Little Red Pen Fiction Editing

ISBN: 978-0-692-04937-2

On Both Banks

Clarence L Harper IV

Dedicated to Toby and Virginia

Acknowledgements

There are many people to thank who had a hand in this book.

First and foremost, I wish to thank my friend and mother-in-law, Doris Waggoner. Thank you for sharing stories with me, and for believing in my work.

To my beta readers, Mark, Eli, Ray, Stacy, and Stephen, and my editor, Lori. This story would never have never crawled out of the primordial ooze of ideas without your time and feedback. I cannot thank you enough.

There is my loving and supportive wife Stephanie, my best friend and co-conspirator, who encouraged me to start writing. My long-suffering parents, CL and Kellye, who had the wherewithal to not kill and eat my brother and I as teenagers. Then there are my poor and pitiable friends who have suffered through my incessant storytelling over the years. How you all put up with me and my rambling all this time is beyond me, but I am so glad you did.

Then there are those non-human inspirations I would be remiss not to mention. Thanks to Friend Crow, who adopted us when I was young and made us part of his life for a time, Einstein, my canine little brother growing up, and my little buddy Pete, the axolotl that helps me remember that weird is normal.

Thanks also go to the burnt-out tree stump in the field next to our first home, the low moaning wind from the Devil's Icebox at Devil's Den State Park, and the whispering howls and crackles of shortwave radio, slowly tuned across the bands in an empty house at three in the morning.

Thank you.

Contents

Contents

Preface

The seeds of this book were sown twenty years ago in a small town south of Seattle. There was a tiny art import store I would visit when I was looking for gifts. The woodwork they sold from Bali, Thailand, and Vietnam was amazing.

On returning from a recent purchasing trip, the owner put a sculpture on display in the showroom that was both beautiful and horrific. It was simultaneously corpulent and emaciated, cadaverous, yet animate. It was wreathed in carved forms of flaming blades and choking vines. At its feet sat a small, ghoulish imp with baleful eyes, and the whole nightmarish assemblage was topped with the head of an elephant, who stared out menacingly from behind razor-barbed tusks.

"Is… is that supposed to be Ganesha?" I stammered in disbelief.

"Yup." The owner's son said. He then pointed to the demonic figure in the corner, with its head full of horns, serpentine tongue, and flaming eyes. "And that there is Jesus."

"The carvers in the villages we buy from, they say 'Evil spirits are scary, so your guy's gotta be scarier.'"

Whether this is correctly representative of any Balinese belief, I do not know, but the idea stuck with me. As I started to write short stories around the theme of 'dreams', I liked the idea that the terrifying nightmare monsters you see in your dreams actually stand between you and something much, much worse. This formed the basis for the stories that eventually became *On Both Banks*.

To be clear. This is a work of fiction. A lie cut from whole cloth. I wouldn't want to cause offense by drawing inappropriate parallels to persons living, dead, or otherwise.

Faceless

She is your sister, but not your actual sister. She is a dream person. Within the context of the dream you understand that she is your closest family, though the things she says, the things she does, bear no relation to the girl you grew up with. You try to fix her face in your mind, but her features are as impermanent as ripples on a pond.

She has been with you all your life. Today, she is just along for the ride. On another night, she says things just to make you angry while yet on another night she holds you as you cry. She is a faceless sibling, sharing joy and sorrow and turmoil as you sleep.

She is your sister.

She is faceless.

When you tell others about her, you recall only a thing she did, or a thing she said. You gloss over the fact that you know who she is, though you can never recognize her. You skip the feeling of familiarity, even though you have never met her before.

Your faceless sister.

When you relive the fire, or the breakup, or the Christmas when the aliens invaded and Grandma turned into a porcupine, or you are standing in the kitchen, which is also a parking garage and your first-grade classroom, she is with you. She smooths the incongruities of time and space and feelings. She lets you say what you need to say. She helps you do what you need to do, even when fear and convention make you tremble.

She is there for you. She is your sister.

When you wake, where does she go? Does she linger, telling her faceless friends about her sibling's strife? Does she recede into memory, a part of you seeking familiarity, all the while goading you further into your own psyche? Perhaps she slumps forward, a marionette put to rest, as a writing form slips out the back of the puppet theater, proud of the show it put on.

Such questions do not linger long though, do they? After all, she is your sister. You can always count on her being there, night after night, as you try to maneuver the whimsical and threatening landscapes you have walked every night since childhood.

Your faceless sister.

If you met her on the street, do you think you would recognize her? Would it be her voice that gives her away? Perhaps the rhythm of her speech? More likely, it would be the way you can't quite fit her features together in your mind. How did her nose curve into her cheeks? How did the corners of her eyes move as she talked?

Are you sure you didn't meet her today, but forgot her already?

After all, she is always there for you.

She is your faceless sister.

6

Samantha

"Why Skulls?"

Samantha opened one bleary eye and tried to focus on her daughter. Carla stood by the bed wearing her daddy's Lakers t-shirt as a nightgown, and an angry pout instead of her usual smile.

It had been a long day between the car breaking down, the call to the IRS, and the worst hay fever in Samantha's adult life. She just wanted to sleep. For the love of God, any god would do, was that really too much to ask? What was it now?

"Skulls are dumb. Why do they all look like skulls?"

Samantha looked past her daughter into the empty doorway. She closed her eyes and stared through the shadowed dim to the silhouette of a lone geist quivering just outside her room. Its glowing, jawless skull emoted fear, like a kid about to get busted for stealing cookies.

Samantha snarled, frightening the haunt back down the hall.

"He figured you'd do that." Carla sighed with a hint of smugness as she crawled into her parent's bed. "So why do they look like skulls?"

There was a lot to unpack in that question. In parenting classes, you are told to acknowledge imaginary friends, but to always reinforce that they are make believe. It was okay to visit the land of make believe, but you couldn't live there. Unfortunately, her daughter's question suggested that she knew what she saw, and a simple dismissal would not suffice. Carla was a sharp girl. So much like her grandma, rest her soul.

Samantha shook off the fuzziness of the allergy medicine and hoisted herself upright. She smiled at her daughter as she lifted the girl into her lap, running her fingers through her hair.

"Okay, so what have you seen, girl?"

"What you just saw."

Samantha smiled, hoping it would come through in her voice. "I don't know that I saw anything."

Carla groaned. "Yeah, they said you'd say that."

"Who's they?"

Carla groaned in irritation. "Nobody... Whatever... I—"

"Okay, okay, baby, it's okay. It's alright. Now, why don't we start at the beginning. Hmm? That's a good girl. Now why don't you tell your mamma what happened before you came in here?"

Carla let out a huff. "Fine. I was lying in bed singing and another skull ghost came out of the curtains. It came out of the curtains and wrung its hands before just floating next to the bed. I said, 'Go away!' I said, 'Jesus says you have to go away,' and it sorta looked sad and just wrung its hands like it wanted to say something, but just floated there looking worried."

"So this has happened before, huh?"

Carla shrugged a little.

"When'd this first happen?"

Carla shrugged. "I dunno, after Auntie Kay left."

Realization dawned quickly. Samantha pursed her lips and winked back the sting in her own eyes.

"Did your auntie teach you a special song, baby? Something to sing when you were scared?"

"Yeah. She said to practice it. She said to 'keep it in my heart.'"

Samantha turned her daughter toward her and held her close. "I bet you those little ghosts are hearing that song and thinking 'Now there's a little girl that can sing. Somebody must love her a whole lot to teach her that kind of singing!' I bet you that's why they come. But only at night, right?"

Carla nodded.

"Well, if you wanna practice your auntie's song, how about you do it during the day, baby. And at night, you only sing that song if you get scared like your aunt Kay said, okay? Then you won't have to be seeing those skull ghosts or whatever."

She lifted Carla and carried her daughter back into her darkened bedroom. All around, Samantha could sense the shadows moving, cowering behind toys and bedroom furniture. She closed her eyes and gazed about from empty lidless sockets. All around, small, luminous eyes darted away, trying to avoid the dread gaze of the Gatekeeper carrying the small girl.

Her daughter had unwittingly called them, and not just one or two responded, but a whole army of tiny nightmares. Somewhere within her, Samantha's pride of her girl, and her fears for her, hid themselves away from her sight.

"Okay! Okay! Mamma Samantha Johnson is in the house. Everything's good. Y'all can go on home! Everything is A-Okay here! You got that?"

The room was still.

Samantha tucked Carla into bed and turned up the 'sleepy time' mix on her daughter's music player.

"There we go, honey. You sleep tight, munchkin, okay?"

"Okay, Mamma."

Samantha stealthily turned on the baby monitor as she backed out of the room.

From the bed, a little voice raised.

"Mamma, you never answered my question."

"What's that?"

"Why are they always skulls?"

Samantha rolled her eyes in the dark. "I dunno, baby. If I see one, I'll ask it, alright?"

"Mmm-hmm..."

Samantha smiled at her daughter from the dim of the hallway. "Okay, shhh... try to go to sleep."

Samantha took three paces down the hall and sniffed. She followed the non-smell to the kitchen and closed her eyes as she dropped onto all fours. In the dark, her six empty eyes lit up with a pale light, and a small skull-faced vapor luminesced with a prismatic sheen from behind the doors of the lower cabinets.

"Okay little one," the Gatekeeper snarled, trying to make the growl of her voice as gentle as she could. "She called. You came. But from who? Where?"

Hiding was no use, but the spirit remained frozen behind the doors. "It Flays The Threads Of Knitted Flesh! It knows our name. We must answer the Bounder's song. Please... Please don't eat us."

Samantha—the thing that the waking world knew as Samantha—laid upon the floor, her massive crocodilian skull cocked to one side to create the hint of a smile.

"My daughter is no Bounder. The one whose song she sings—that the girl here sings. Is that who you answer to? What is her status?"

"It Flays The Threads Of Knitted Flesh stands on both banks, Gatekeeper, most sinister of visage!"

Relief filled Samantha's heart. Kay still lived, in some form or another. Bless her soul, you'd think she had never heard of a phone before.

"Well, you have answered the call. Do you serve my daughter now?"

"May We?"

Samantha snarled lightly. "Ask her yourself. Gain a voice, watch from the shadows, and only come when you're called. Then perhaps she will accept you."

"If not? It Flays The Threads Of Knitted Flesh was clear. If We do not serve, We..."

"You will not be cast from the shadows of this house."

The small shade filtered out through the gaps in the cabinet and coalesced nervously.

"Thank you, Gatekeeper, most sinister of visage, We..."

"*You* had better find a good place to sleep and stay out of trouble, sugar. It's been a long night, and I don't got time for any more trouble."

The specter backed away, bowing profusely and muttering thanks as it slipped into a heater vent in the corner.

Samantha hefted herself onto her shaggy hindquarters and opened her eyes. She looked at the clock hopefully, but it was already 4:00am. She was so tired she wanted to cry, but simply shook her head. She reached over and flipped on the coffee maker. As bread crisped in the toaster, she poured her first cup of joe and greeted the day, with its familiar smells.

The Monitor

The Monitor clicked the remote from one channel to the next, watching for images that matched the sounds from the speakers too closely to be coincidental.

Infomercial audio being spoken by some sort of snake-dog-demon.

Click

Sounds from an adult film forming the soundtrack of racing through the mountains on a motorcycle.

Click

More infomercial announcers, this time narrating a desolate, blighted landscape.

Click

Another infomercial, for plastic knives, from an angry preacher covered in bees.

Click

The many-headed bat creature had been doing this for hours, with no relief in sight. This sort of surveillance could get monotonous at times. You used to be able to rely on channels eventually going off the air for the night, but now, thanks to cable TV and autoplay videos on the internet, there were so many more hazards for the wayward dreamers to stumble upon. So to speak.

Frank Sinatra. On fire. New Delhi fire services en route to the blaze.

Click

Harrison Ford explaining car insurance to elderly cab drivers in Kansas.

Click

Japanese pop music and a South American woman baking bread.

Click

Santa Claus... singing opera.

He paused and watched, padded finger hovering over the remote. The Santa's face was lit from below, with a vague menace in the eyes. And the opera? Don Giovani. The iconic Commendatore scene. Santa's movements were those of a practiced performer. This was no case of the human mind trying to make sense of the things it heard while it slept. No, this was a threat to someone who may have strayed beyond the safety of their bed.

The Monitor lowered itself slowly from where it hanged in its perch, like a spider descending on its prey, and extended one grasping finger into the television screen. It pulled its leathery wings tight to its body and shimmied into the nightmare already in progress.

John knew nothing of opera, but he knew a real bad thing when he saw it. Santa Claus stood over him, a stern and horrible grin on his waxy face. He could not understand the words being sung at him, but the message was clear. John was about to die.

Moments ago, he'd been shooting hoops behind the school where he went to prom. He was talking with some bros about the girls and—or no, wait, he was there with some girls, and he was trying to get their phone numbers. Then they had started singing and he just went with it. He walked hand-in-hand with one to a fancy restaurant.

They were just having their appetizer when Santa Claus came out of the kitchen singing in a mighty baritone.

"A cenar tecom'invitasti e son venuto,"

Santa grinned menacingly. John couldn't breathe. He was trapped in the gaze of those yellow-green eyes.

"Rispondimi: verrai tu a cenar meco?"

John tried to scream, but the dead face of Father Christmas loomed in close to his. The breath smelled like rotting milk.

John tried to be brave, He tried to yell at this monster, but all that came out was a squeaking hiss of "I'm not afraid... not of..."

Santa's smile got bigger at those words, and he grabbed John's hand.

"Consent," he demanded.

It didn't sound like that is what he sang, but that's how John heard it. His response was a strained squeak. He couldn't have agreed to anything even if he tried. His heart pounded in his chest, and his entire world was framed by the worm-filled beard and ashen flesh of Saint Nick rotting before his eyes. He tried to break free, yelling "No! No!" but with every pull and twist, the grip on his arm and his chest grew tighter.

Then there was a hellish chord, and a hundred voices sang out at once in a harsh, dissonant tone. The rotting face pulled back into darkness, and John fell back, screaming, spinning to the floor of...

Larry's Drive-N-Dine.

It was the diner John had worked at during college. That one chick he couldn't stand was here, Cynthia, leaning over him and offering her hand.

"You're supposed to be mopping up spills, not becoming one, you goof! C'mon."

John laughed. It was busy lunch shift, and the place was packed. He dashed to his next table, where he was sitting down with Cynthia. It was ten years later, and now it was their first dinner together as man and wife. Now it was the drive back from the hospital, Cynthia holding their first daughter. Now it was the crayon marks on the wall, and the toddler blaming it on her friend, the giant fruit bat monster that lives in the attic.

Far above, in the shadowed rafters and boughs of the dream, the many faces of the bat-like Monitor bit and gnawed at the horror concealed in its leathery wings. It waited until the dreamer drifted away, hopefully with no memory of what had just passed.

The dreamer woke, and the vignette unfolded as the dream reabsorbed into The Manifold. The Monitor tarried his way home, slinking from one impossible space to the next. The Gatekeepers did not let things this big, this tasty, just slip through. They would have to be alerted, of course, but surely they would not begrudge a mere Monitor taking the time to savor its meal.

Initiation

Father Lucas Martin Francis clutched his pillow to his face as though it could bung the hole in his soul. He prayed that it wasn't true. Everything he was, or thought he was, depended on the omnipotence and omnibenevolence of The Father, the Divinity of his Son, the Grace of the Holy Spirit, and the benevolent intercession of the Saints. He prayed, begged, that he was not losing his faith. He prayed aloud between his tears, but the words left him hollow, further driving his sorrow.

His ship had been sinking for many years, part of him knew. He had been a priest most of his life. He had been an integral part of his community, and taken the confessions of so many people, each unburdening to him the weight on their souls that they might once again be able to return to His good graces. He had seen weddings and funerals and christenings across cultures and generations. He was looked to for stability and comfort during times of fear and social unrest. In him, the congregation sought something like a reflection of God's love.

Father Francis, however, could only feel the weight of the suffering. He made a study of the martyrs. He sought out the words of his namesake and tried to emulate his simple universal compassion, only to discover it wasn't simple at all. Try as he might, it took far more strength than Lucas possessed to be as gentle and resolved as that.

He started to wonder if any person could be.

He started to wonder if even God could be that compassionate.

Or if compassion was even a divine quality.

He had always dismissed the question, "Is there a God?" as one of the ignorant or the provocateur. Of course there is a God.

His works abound. You have merely to open yourself to his gifts.

Then Lucas started looking around and wondering where those gifts were. In his parish, most the congregation was poor. The Church helped them take care of the costs of food for their children, but the parents often had few prospects for work. Mental health issues abounded, with nobody willing or able to address treatments. Even the small fraction of the families that were a little better situated faced horrible struggles with their health issues, legal troubles, or fear for the future of mankind.

Then, after thirty-six years, came the morning when he stood before his congregation, looked out across the weary faces, and wept. He tried to carry out his devotional duties, but his sorrow was visible, and his fellow priest, Father Duncan, edged in to take over as Francis slid out the access door behind the altar.

After mass, Father Duncan eventually found him in the alley behind the church, a stale cigarette in his hands and a vacant look in his eyes.

Duncan sat next to him, but the senior priest was unresponsive. Duncan had seen this before in his own mother, and said nothing. He merely took the smoldering cigarette from Francis's hand, took a slow drag off of it, and handed it back to his fellow clergyman.

They sat there beside the dumpster for almost an hour, staring at the blank wall across from them. Francis eventually stood, patted Duncan on the shoulder, and walked away, taking his collar off and sliding it into the pocket of his slacks.

Officially, Father Francis was simply on sabbatical. He was scheduled to be back 'soon', or 'in a while', or 'down the road'. Father Duncan checked in with him at his apartment twice a day, concerned whether he had actually eaten anything or bathed. Duncan was scared that he might come in and find Lucas the way he'd found his own mother, and prayed that this sudden turn in his friend and mentor would not lead to the same heartbreaking end.

Father Francis, merely Lucas now, lay in bed for days, staring at the thickly textured stucco on the wall. Time was measured in shades of gray as the darkness of the apartment ebbed and flowed like a tide.

Weeks had passed, and in his stupor Lucas didn't register the sound at his door. Not at first. It was a scraping sound barely louder than the bathroom fan. It would go for several minutes, then stop, only to start again. Its dull grating quality found its way deep into Lucas's brain and caused him to grit his teeth.

He stood sharply, threw his bathrobe around himself, and flung open the door to his apartment. Seeing nobody there, he took one step out to find the source, only to brush his foot against something warm and wet.

It was a cat, badly injured. Blood covered its fur and its breathing was labored.

Lucas reached down and touched the poor thing, and as if through reflex, began to give it last rites. He paused abruptly and his face turned hard and defiant. He plunged back into his apartment, returning with a blanket, a box, and his slippers.

He held the box close to him on the bus, talking to the injured cat inside. He wanted to pray. The need was overwhelming, but who would be there to hear it? He was at a loss. He looked around, and saw the people trying not to notice the wild-haired, middle-aged man in slippers and a Garfield bathrobe talking to a box. For a moment he started to grow self-conscious, but then came a weak mewing from within the box, and his world again focused on the suffering creature in his lap.

He returned home that night, his hands still stained in blood. The vets weren't sure whether the cat would live. Being a stray, we'll probably need to put it down. No, no, I'll pay the bill, do what you can. Thank you, Doctor. Thank you, Father Francis.

Father Duncan and a police officer were waiting in his kitchen when he returned. Duncan had seen the blood, and being as Lucas was... under a lot of strain. Kitten. Obviously, you understand the concern. Gash in the neck. Sir, have you been having any thoughts of hurting yourself? The blanket, soaked in blood, fur matted with clots. No officer. It was a stray cat. Veterinary emergency. I'm fine.

Lucas was up all night. As he paced, he imagined the cat laying in the dark, the monotonous rhythm of a respirator pulsing, air heavy with an acrid antiseptic smell. This was the hospital room of every child that had died in his presence. It was the Viaticum delivered at the behest of one who knew they were going to pass, even when the doctor and the family did not. It was the homeless man who lied and said he was Catholic just so someone would be in the room with him when he died. Now all of them, they were all bound up in the delicate life of an injured cat.

Lucas could hear Padre Angelo taking confession. Lucas stood in the narthex of St Basil's, then only a choirboy. It was Tuesday, and he worked cleaning the church with his mother. He heard the angry voice and pounding from the confessional. He saw the wild eyes and the shirtless man yelling about the Antichrist, Jews, and Freemasons storming out into the street, right into the path of a rather surprised cop who had been walking up the sidewalk.

Padre Angelo had conversed with the officer. No charges. Please get him help. Thank you. God Bless you. Angelo's melodic baritone voice carried such compassion, it was hard to imagine him angry or shaken.

As he walked back inside, he paused and laid a calloused hand on Lucas's shoulder. "There's no saving the world, my son." His eyes had a hint of sorrow, a sorrow that moved Lucas even now. "We only do what we can to save each other."

Lucas turned and watched Father Angelo walk away, pulled along by thick luminous cords that seemed to pass out of him and through him.

Lucas shook the image, and was again waiting. At a bed, in a waiting room, at the scene of an accident. Always, someone coming into this world, or leaving it behind forever. Always, he was a bystander. He made his entrance, said his words, and stepped away as part of the chorus.

So many times, he felt there was something more he could have done. Should have done. The accidents he drove past on the freeway when he was younger, how might they have played out if he had stopped? The man yelling incoherently and wandering in traffic when he visited Chicago. What happened to him? Who was the dark figure that approached him and talked him out of the street?

In all his years of being a priest, he saw no angels. He saw no intercession of saints. What he saw were miracles performed by those that decided to act on behalf of complete strangers. That was the devotion to the Word that inspired tales of miracles. It wasn't mysticism or signs that made a saint, it was the actions they performed. Even beyond the grave, after earning their rest, their love and devotion guided them to intercede among the living. It was not because of any kind of faith in them, but due to their burning compassion that they had no choice but to do *something*.

Lucas looked up and found himself standing in a small garden surrounded by dark shadows. Before him stood a quiet man in simple robes. He smiled gently. He seemed familiar. A small bird landed upon his shoulder, dragging with it a luminous thread which the gentle man took from the tiny beak and offered to Lucas. Lucas took the thread and held it to his chest as though he was holding a child to his heart. He felt warmth flooding through him. There was sorrow and hardship, yes, but there was also joy. He could feel the life tied to the other end of the thread, and wanted more for it than he had ever wanted for himself.

The feeling consumed him, and he held out his other hand. The gentle man smiled and produced from his robes a bundle of glowing, scintillating threads, each trailing off into the dim. Lucas grabbed them to his chest, holding them as close as possible, until it seemed like they—

He woke with a start as the phone rang. Sometime during his reverie sleep had crept up on him, and he launched himself from the couch to where he had left his phone in the kitchen. The only thing he remembered of the call were the words 'gonna be alright'. The rest were mere details. He dressed quickly, being sure to leave a note for Father Duncan should he visit, and hopped the bus to the shelter.

They took him into the recovery kennel. The small tabby lay there, exhausted. Huge sections of her body had been shaved so they could treat her multiple lacerations. The cat is chipped, but the owner has been dead for months. If nobody claims it we'll have to... why yes, I guess he was part of your parish. I don't think releasing her to you would be a problem. Let's give her a few days to recover though. Name? The chip says Therese, but you could name her whatever you want.

Lucas and the attendant stepped out of the recovery area. He looked out and saw rows of kennels, heard the whimpers and barks and plaintive moans. He felt in that moment a sharp pull in his chest.

"Excuse me," he said past the lump in his throat, "But, how much does it take to care for these animals each month? Do... do you need volunteers?"

No More Distractions

Chris had spent the last couple of years haunting new-age bookstores. She had cycled through all the pre-packaged, re-costumed quasi-Jungian pseudo paganisms on the shelves. Some had a resonance, a clear note from an outer chime, but it was dampened by Pablum and drek. She haunted the library, reading the Romantics, the works of The Enlightenment, and the counterculture heroes of the 1960's like Leary, Kesey, and Wilson but she was met with frustration. They all had some luminous edge to them, but each was muddled and incoherent in their own special way.

She decided to seek out the root material, and studied the older religions, and those that she had only a passing under-standing of. She delved into Hinduism, Zoroastrianism, Buddhism, and Zen with-out Zen Masters. She annoyed friends, routed family, and stamped in frustration at every expert or theologian that claimed witness to a singular grand revelation. Every shelf in her house was stocked with the accounts of unreliable narrators, all of whom had some sort of intrinsic or ecstatic experience, gleaned some sliver of insight from it, then walled it up in a castle made of utter bullshit.

When she closed her eyes, she fought the ideas. They were ninjas and samurai, barbarians and knights. They swung swords and axes and whips and chains, lashing out her and at each other. At the same time, they were like microbes in a petri dish, locked in an eternal struggle of eat or be eaten. Warriors or microbes, Chris found herself standing in the midst of the raging battle, looking toward the horizon. There was something there. Past the melee there was something luminous; a light eclipsed by sword and shield and flying bodies. Every night, she picked her way through the battle, only to lose sight of it in between the gouts of blood and flashing metal.

Then she would wake, still feeling the ache of muscles worn by combat and the scent of blood in her nostrils. These only served to annoy her further. She stopped interacting with friends and colleagues, as she worried she would be surly toward them and hurt their feelings. She worried they would say something inane or incorrect and that she would lash out at them, layering context on context until they were sorry they had come.

So she buried herself in work, which was barely a distraction from the battle raging in her head.

She had gone to the library earlier and saw a little girl wearing a strange hooded sweatshirt. It was long and printed like Alice from *Alice in Wonderland*, but the sleeves and hood had a metallic diamond-shaped print that suggested chainmail armor. Chris followed the girl at a distance as she wandered the stacks, until she at last ran into the arms of her mother. Mom was the same age as Chris, and looked like a young Shelley Duvall with spikey green hair and a heavy gauge nose ring. She was conversing with a stately elderly gentleman wearing an impeccable vintage suit. He knelt down to the little girl and gave her a hug. She, in turn, hugged him, then turned and pointed at Chris.

All three looked at her.

Chris froze. It was that moment when the viewer discovers that they are the viewee. The little Alice must have realized she was being followed, came to Mom and Grandpa, and now Chris was some creepy lady stalking children through the stacks. Ew!

The little girl waved, and Mom, with a smile, led the girl away toward the circulation desk. The gentleman stayed behind, watching after them, shooting the occasional smile to Chris. It took her a moment to realize that he was waiting for her benefit, and so she approached despite her embarrassment.

"You know," he said, his voice surprisingly feminine and tenor, "everyone thinks they have the road map. You turn here, you do this dance, memorize this handshake, and you'll get where you're going."

Chris frowned, her shoulders going slack, "Yeah, but it doesn't work that way."

The fellow sighed, a wry grin on his lips and brow. "No, no it doesn't. Sailors knew this, of course. Can't map the waves, you know. So they set their sights on the stars. Of course, they needed to know something about where they wanted to go to know which stars to follow, but those stars were beyond the waves, and beyond the weather. They were there night after night. So the Polynesians knew. So the Greeks and the Chinese knew. You can fill your cabin with enough maps to get yourself well and truly lost, but with a few stars, why, you can know where you are, and find your way anywhere. Well, at night, at least."

Chris stared at the man, but he simply gave her a nod just shy of a hat tip and wandered off toward the reference section. She stood there, a little incredulous. It dawned on her that if she didn't catch up to him and find out more about who he was, then she would be living the 'wise old stranger appears out of nowhere' cliché and there was no way she would accept that.

She trotted off after him, only to find he had vanished among the atlases and encyclopedias.

Chris stamped her feet angrily, growling as loud as her self-consciousness would permit in a library, and raced home in a huff.

No more distractions! Tonight was the night. This world was but a flimsy shadow of a greater reality and tonight she would push out beyond it. She was a traveler on a sea of maps. Maps and bodies. But she had her star, and she would reach the further shore. Yes, this would happen!

She lay in bed, full of excitement and determination, but wide-awake. The shadows in the room lengthened and faded as evening turned to night, and night passed seamlessly to dawn. Through all the long hours, she never slept.

In the pre-dawn glow, she lay wide-eyed, staring at her bookshelves, and sighed.

Enough maps to get yourself well and truly lost.

Shit.

She sat up and stared about her room. Maslow, Rumi, Augustine in this pile. Lao-Tzu, Paine, Machiavelli and Derrida over there in the corner. She had built a huge map of the human experience, overlaying text on text until the whole structure was damn near impermeable. Just like the writers she had long criticized, she had seen a sliver of truth, and had built a castle of bullshit around it. No—worse than that, she had seen a descriptive fragment saying that there was a sliver of truth, and then built a hovel of pig slop around that.

Shit.

"There is no grand revelation, is there?" she asked her book-infested room. "There is just an ecosystem of ideas and sudden shifts in perspective that seem profound. There is no garden of gods and immortal truth, we're just petri dishes, cross-contaminating each other with riddles, hoping to solve for X, when X is really just our own dissatisfaction and fear."

The books were silent.

Hearing those words come from her mouth saddled her with both disappointment and great relief. It was like being sober after a bender, or coming home after a long vacation. Everything familiar now felt vaguely foreign. She dressed, and went for a walk as the rhythms of the new day played out across her neighborhood. These too seemed foreign to her, but she knew she would adjust to them. For the first time in many years, she felt like she had finally woken up.

The great monster, The Teeth Beneath The Dark River, withdrew her talons from the dream, massaging the glowing membrane back into seamless calm. Hopefully that would keep the girl doubting. She was far too concrete to make it across the river without suffering, but by that same token, it didn't feel right letting the lights of other dreams continue to entice the girl from across the darkness. Hopefully now she could find some rest and even think she arrived at her destination by following her own star, as it were. Cheesy and cliché, perhaps, but The Teeth Beneath The Dark River had never been one for nautical metaphors.

Raw Data

As a pup, the Monitor might have taken time to pontificate. Humans, the kind that found their way here, always described everything as something else. They described the Monitor's home as being like an infinite library, a many-angled labyrinth, or an ever-expanding fractal of sensations with an underlying alien logic beyond fathoming.

To hear them talk about it was agonizingly... weird. Humans could be right there in the same relational space as the Monitor, interacting with the underpinnings of co-sensual liminal space as the Monitor did, but somehow, something in their mind meat turned the whole experience into something else. For humans, 'What I am experiencing' never became 'What I have experienced'. It was always transformed into an amorphous, indistinct facsimile of something familiar, but somehow not. The experience would become something like running through a forest, tending a control room, or rutting in a graveyard. If a particular human possessed a broad experience set and had been here before, they might go so far as describing the Monitor's home as an N-th dimensional non-orientable gestalt data construct born of the convoluted needs of the collective subconscious of all sentient life.

The Monitor would shrug its wings and smile weakly from its many bat-like faces.

If anything operated under unfathomable alien logics, it was humans.

The thought slipped away as quickly as did the blurs of color-sound around it, as the Monitor scanned across time for seemingly unrelated moments. No screens to mediate the experience tonight. It needed to see the shape of the raw data, to taste the coarse curvatures of cause and effect between its padded fingers.

From its narrow, highly abstracted vantage, using mental algorithms that simulated human metaphoric thought, the

Monitor had seen what looked like a trend. It had grown lean, and it appeared there were less Hungering Things making their way deep into The Manifold. The Monitor adjusted the size of the data set, but there were no concentrations or patterns, just a slowing population trend over time. All the while the Bounders, those humans that go where nobody is supposed to go, reported many, many more Hungering Things than they had witnessed before. Sadly, Bounders were just as prone to metaphoric thinking as other humans. They could tell you what they saw, what they did, and where they were, but rarely all three at the same time. Not to the degree that it generated a reliable data point.

So, stripping away the abstractions, the Monitor dove into the data, the live data, scanning the 'Now' set as rapidly as it could before it could become a 'Then'. The Monitor held its wings wide, feeling the shape of the color-sounds as it tumbled and crawled over the local set labeled 'Earth'.

As it raced through the data, a single note, a ping, emitted from its many mouths. It was a query—the very shape and pitch of the note a request and a demand, only created to reach its intended recipients. In turn, those recipients would answer back, whether they realized it or not.

The Monitor replayed the data, passing back over the 'Now' set at intervals, feeling for responses. From across the data, scintillating echoes flared up. Every one of them was a Bounder, and most of them far from the edges of The Manifold, engaged with both dreamers and Hungering Things alike.

As the Monitor feared, the dreamers were where the Hungering Things were. Not the other way around.

It grimaced, and sought through the 'Now' set for someone to warn. This was the sort of important revelation you miss if you rely solely on abstraction. Of course, without an idea of what you are looking for, the raw data set could be as useless as it is overwhelming. It is no wonder the others could not have known this was happening. They were, most of them, humans, once or currently. They work under alien logics, after all.

The Monitor thought quickly. Bounders get around, but there are too many, and not all would be asleep and engaged right now. Guardians know that their wards would be terrified of the Monitor, and so it didn't want to just appear before them. Then there were the Gatekeepers, who on further consideration were just best left alone. This was different, though. This was of critical import, and the Monitor puzzled how to reach them all as quickly as possible. It considered doing a mass insert of the data for all 'incursive mind' entities, but that would be rude at best, and could have violently damaging repercussions. He could pin the information to something as all-encompassing as inertia or energy conservation, but that might be too subtle, and the information could be lost in plain sight.

Ancestors! Those ancient and revered... things. They did not exist in the 'Now' data set. None of the data sets, really, but where there were missing fields and unfilled pointers, you could find an instance of them intersecting the set of 'All Things'.

The monitor pinged for null values and invalid pointers. In the 'Now' set he found three similarly oriented data forms. A half-asleep young girl holding an envelope to her chest, a young man sitting at a fountain next to a cloaked nightmare, and a small forest shade sleeping between the toes of a hellish monster. The common thread? A series of null values forming a familiar cross section in the data.

The Monitor clenched its many teeth, knowing how bad this was going to hurt, and folded the null points over each other. Holding them together as a temporary sub-set, it unfolded its mind into the empty fields, showing as much as telling what the Monitor had seen while examining the Bounder query.

The physical sensation was wonderful and horrible. It was like violent regurgitation, yet fundamentally different. It was agonizingly... weird. For a moment, the Monitor had an appreciation of what its human counterparts suffered trying to relate to the raw data.

Introductions

The veil looked like tormented faces, flowing and swirling from one horrified appearance to another. Their voices, a howling wind of anguish, grew stronger as Samantha felt her way along the obscured rocky path. There had been a call, something like the scent of home crossed with the low notes of an avalanche, and there was no resisting it.

Angry hands felt as if they tore at her clothes and the sounds of her own fears rang in her ears, but she pressed on toward the brilliant glow of the beacon.

As she neared, details of the hands and faces faded into undifferentiated shadow. Samantha stepped into the outer edges of a campfire's light and waited. Before her was a collection of nightmares, haunts, and outer beasts the likes of which Samantha had never seen, assembled in one place. She smiled broadly and sloughed off her human guise. She kicked her daily-wear skin back behind a tree and shambled toward the fire, the light glinting brightly off her many teeth.

Her eyes met with the many faces of an angry mob whose uniforms shifted in color and fashion. The many faces smiled at her and beckoned her forward, a chorus of voices greeting her. "Aaaaaah! Welcome! I was wondering if we were in your neighborhood!"

The Teeth Beneath The Dark River forgot all about being Samantha and squealed girlishly as she lumbered into the mob. They, in turn, laughed and collapsed upon her in a group hug. She had been so terrified of him, but he was her first teacher, and as time passed, she had come to understand his terrible job.

"How are you? It is a busy night, yes? Are you on duty?"

Teeth backed away, laughing. "No, yes, good! This doesn't look like an emergency,

The Angry Calls Of A Distant Many. Is there an occasion?"

"It's 'The Calls of Many' now," the faces beamed. "I've had to adopt other roles, and now I am the army that stands at your back, as you stare down that which you will defeat. I still keep up on the horror of the angry crowd, but—well, there's enough of that in the world without my help."

They exchanged knowing glances and Calls gestured to the fire. "Please, take a seat. Sorry to be so rude! Everybody, this is my friend, The Teeth Beneath The Dark River. Teeth, you may be familiar with a few here, we have Baskerville, Shadowdog, and Buster. They are old childhood terrors that have recently emancipated and have joined in the hunt."

The three canine forms looked like they were made of pure shadow, with glowing eyes and teeth that glinted brightly in the firelight. Two of the dark mastiffs sniffed at her and wagged their tails while the third one, a tall nightmare with the flowing profile of a giant Afghan hound, cowered slightly.

"We've met..." Baskerville whimpered.

"Oh? Oh, yes, I guess we have." The Teeth Beneath The Dark River smiled, trying to let the warmth of her voice mellow the fixed expression of her face.

"I'm sorry, Gatekeeper. I was... I was just..."

"Feeding. I know. It's okay now. No hard feelings, I mean it. That's right..." She reached out her talons and brushed the nightmare's head gently.

Calls smiled and continued, gesturing to the huge, toad-like man dressed in tattered sheets. He was proportioned like a fat Bodi statue made of mud and sticks. He bowed gently, creaking out "Someone Died There Once, my pleasure."

Teeth bowed in turn.

Then there was the bird. In size and color it was like a brilliant red Macaw, but it had a radiance that sent rainbows dancing across her scales and bone and fur. It was an Ancestor. Teeth fell to all fours and tried to look away, but she could feel the Ancestor stare through her and smile.

Teeth tried to speak, but she had no control over her words. She felt herself reciting a prayer, a lyric of gratitude of which she had no memory of ever having heard. When she looked up, the Ancestor was gone. She could remember nothing of the many things they said to each other. Calls, standing next to the empty seat, smiled. "And then, over here, we have..."

Introductions went all round, but Teeth was still lost in the presence of the Ancestor. Her heart was full, and for the first time since losing her waking job, her heart felt light.

The fire burned, and as usual at these gatherings, small geists and shades wandered in from the dark. They were drawn like moths to the light of the fire, enduring the insatiable terrors of the veil that shrouded the camp. They had now seen too much, but had been drawn ever forward to the beacon. And now, having passed through their own agony, they stood before entities that could, and should, devour them in a heartbeat. They were ready to hunt the emanations of The City.

Teeth remembered first stepping out of fear and into The Manifold. She remembered staring down her tormentors and lashing out with razor teeth and scything talons. She rent the membrane of her personal hell, and found herself staring out across a sea of amber dreams, pulsing and folding in and over each other like a protein. To her right stood Calls, who had long stood in for her childhood abusers, and behind her an Ancestor, bathed in light, throwing fractured rainbows about her where she stood. Teeth knew her duty that day, and took an Oath of Service to stand forever in shadow, keeping The Crushing Dark at bay.

Conversation was brisk among the nightmares. Died There Once took the small geists and shade in around him, giving them something to anchor to amid the boisterous and foreign conversation. The news brought by the ancestor was cause for concern. Dreamers were not straying from the manifold. The other Gatekeepers and Guardians weren't turning more sleepyheads than normal. No, it was like they fell asleep directly into The City, making them easy prey.

Baskerville and the other hounds looked up sharply, hair bristling. Conversation stopped. A faint Bounder's song drifted through the veil and circled in the smoke from the fire.

"Mamma!"

She thought she imagined it, but the pulse of a luminous thread shocked her to action. The Teeth Beneath The Dark River bristled and growled fiercely. The geists scattered, and the black dogs fell in behind her, following gleefully as she turned and tore through the veil. As she bounded through The Manifold, the black dogs howled cries of war and death in her wake.

Carla felt the tiny skeletal hand on her arm, shaking her, making pigeon sounds that got louder and louder until she finally awoke. She tried to brush the annoying skull-faced spirit away, but then saw where it was pointing. In the dim, she could see a man leaning over her bed, staring at her. She tried to scream, but she couldn't breathe.

She could only think of her auntie's song. She squeaked out what notes she could, but her voice seized as the man came around the side of Carla's bed. She tried to whistle it, but she had stopped breathing. The annoying little skull ghost look to Carla apologetically, turning into a dark vapor that filled her lungs. With a gasped breath, the notes that issued forth rebuffed the man and spread beyond the edges on her room.

The intruder paused for a moment, dumbstruck. He seemed to listen for a moment, and when no response came from the rest of the house, his panicked expression was replaced by a salacious sneer. His movements were slow and deliberate as he tilted his head and considered her. Carla couldn't move. All she could do was watch, like she was watching a video of him reaching out to pull her blanket away from her.

That is when the door to the room burst in.

Light flooded the room, and the walls unfolded and fell into shadow. As they vanished, three monstrous dogs flanked the bed. The intruder fell backwards, terror stricken. He tried to backstroke along the floor, but came to a stop as his hand struck the talon of a giant beast. It looked like it was made of undead bits of bear and dinosaur. The monster roared, and the intruder stared, dumbstruck, into the gaping maw of death. As the lights went out, the last thing he saw were the enraged eyes of an adult woman and the baseball bat she brought down on his face.

In her mind, she didn't stop beating him for hours. Even as she took the phone from Carla and talked to Gavin at dispatch. She was still beating him as Officers Mercer and Harris came in, saw that the suspect was dead, checked that Carla was alright, and began taking their report. She was still on his chest, rending at his face as the ambulance came to take the body.

As the ambulance left, three dark hounds trailed the ambulance all the way to the hospital, nipping and tearing at the remains of the man it carried.

Carla clung to Samantha all night, and the tiny, skull-faced "Coo Coo" clung to the girl. Samantha sat on the front porch, rocking them both as the sun came up only to drift to sleep with the dawn.

Fireside Interlude

The Teeth Beneath The Dark River lounged on the rock overlooking the camp. It was always fun seeing kids out in the woods. There were many dangers here, but when they closed their eyes, they tended to stray from the safety of their dreams and explore the shadows of The Manifold. It was like watching lion cubs play at hunting, never considering how close they actually were to safety.

Beside her sat a Faceless, her featureless "man-mask" riding atop her head like a jaunty 1940's stewardess cap. She leaned against the boulder, stretching her long, spindly arms in a wide sigh as her drab robes draped across the grass.

"It's good to have a quiet night." The Faceless smiled with shifted feminine features. "Things have been so bad lately.

Kids know it. And ones this age, they're just starting to get a hint, you know?"

Teeth smiled. "Yes. It is good. This is as close as some of them will ever be to both banks. So who are you here for?"

The Faceless pointed lazily. "See the little stoner-looking one. He's been close. He's seen a few things, but I think he's convinced himself it was the drugs. There are Ancestors watching him. I've seen a big heron or crane lurking around, so I don't worry about him. It's his brother, the little blonde one by the fire I worry about. He's got some hurts he's carrying, and I don't know how many he's ever gonna shed."

Teeth spoke sympathetically. "The young girl. The red haired one sitting alone. She does too. I don't know how much more she can take. She can't feel the many threads about her, but good lord, if only she knew how much she was loved."

"You aren't her guardian?"

Teeth shook her head. "She's an acquaintance of my daughter."

The Faceless looked up sharply.

"I know, I know, she's a little too close to be doing this for her, but every shade and geist that has come to her she has either driven off or didn't acknowledge. So, I keep an eye on her and nudge where I can. Once I'm back here on the outside, of course, I have a little more leverage."

The Faceless settled back with an acknowledging sigh.

"You sort of hope they never know. You hope they figure that they figured everything out on their own. Being Faceless, I feel like I am confessor and punching bag. It's hard seeing the shit these kids carry with them."

"Being a kid sucked," Teeth groaned.

"Yeah. Never signing up to do that again."

Songs were sung, and stories told, and the fire waxed and waned. In the darkness beyond the campfire's reach, the two nightmares watched the movements of The

Herder as he passed over the wood like a great luminous cloud. They saw the infinite tiny glowing threads that bound the lives of the forest together, and the human spirits, long since departed, that had made the wild places their home.

Many of the kids began to crawl off to their tents, but the red-haired girl and the little blond boy remained, staring into the dying embers.

They didn't say much, but each slid more and more into themselves, talking as much to the fire and to themselves as to each other. The Faceless smiled.

"It's going to be okay. World's rough, and they'll carry The City with 'em always, but you know, everything's gonna be alright."

Teeth rolled her shoulders side to side, singing "E'ryting's gonna be alright! Mm-mmmm!" in her best Bob Marley impersonation.

"Everthang's gonna be alright!" The Faceless sang along. In the wavering firelight, the two nightmares burst into a sing-a-long rendition of "No Woman, No Cry", complete with flat notes and fuzzy lyrics.

Their mood seemed contagious, and they smiled at each other as they saw The Faceless's ward scoot closer to the red haired girl. When she took his hand in hers, the monsters fell out, missing the lyric and skipping right back to the refrain, "Everything's gonna be alright".

As the fire died, the natural luminance of the forest took hold. The tiny keepers and geists darted from shadow to shadow, while nocturnal foragers picked their way through the dark looking for food. At one point, a deer walked near the boulder, close enough for The Faceless to stroke the animal's flank. The deer leaned in slightly, then continued to poke around the edge of the camp before creeping away from the danger the sleeping humans posed.

"I always did like animals more." Teeth smiled.

"Then why are you doing this?"

"I'm a Gatekeeper, not a Guardian. I'm a game warden. I never said I don't like people. I mean, yeah, folks can be pretty awful. But non-human people, I just like them more."

The Faceless watched the billowing dreams emanating from the tents and adjusted her mask. "You mean like geists and shades?"

"Oh hell yeah." Teeth smiled as she rolled on her back. "I'm not doing this to keep stoners and psychotics from seeing things that will make them write bad poetry or epic rock albums." She pointed to the movements in the woods. "I do this for them. They've been helping us since we first crawled out of the water. This is their world, and they've been willing to share it, but we've been eating it up since we laid bricks and called it Uruk. They've been displaced by The Manifold and hunted by the Hungering Things it attracted. And The City? That's all us. We own that ill. No, when I stepped out and saw the mess we were making, I drew a line at the river. For them, and for the Ancestors, I hold that line."

"I like to see people happy," The Faceless said, wistfully. "I was never visited by Ancestors, that I know of at least. I just... I just realized I could touch someone else's dreams. I realized I could calm the storm, bring comfort, maybe even something like peace to a person."

Teeth rolled back onto her belly and looked up toward the sky, the stars glistening among the dark boughs of pine and cedar. "I think that makes you a better person than me."

"No it doesn't, it—"

"Yeah it does!" Teeth interrupted. "By my standards, you've got the hard job. You wander The Manifold night after night. You see it all. All the joy, all the fears. Hell, probably some kinky shit they don't even have a word for on the Internet."

The Faceless shuddered and laughed. "Ew, yeah, that's why it's good that I can suddenly be the cop-dad-mom-terrorist that breaks the scene. I mean, hell, nobody wants to see that. I'd say, you know, 'get a room', but well, technically they did. Their head, their room. Now I feel kinda bad about it, saying that out loud like that. But only kinda."

"Yeah, that's why you're a better person than me. I'd have been just like, 'Oh hell no, pal. I'm dumping your ass in a parking lot full of clowns and penguins, naked. Let you try to figure that shit out for yourself when you wake up'."

Faceless laughed. "Okay, you win, I'm the better person!"

"That's right, you're the better person, and don't you forget it!"

They sat back in the dark stillness of the woods, watching the dreams of the campers expand and contract, like so many little universes.

It was still dark when the songs of the birds and insects slowly changed, and the gray gloaming brought with it a heavy dew. They could hear the rustling in the tents, and the changes in breathing that said soon there would be coffee and bacon, and slow morning movements.

The Faceless smiled at Teeth with a face that shifted and faded from one set of features to the next. "Looks like my boys are up. I should probably be getting around myself. It's been a real pleasure getting to post up with you."

Teeth nodded. "Yeah, I don't normally get to just hang out. Maybe if those two start dating or something we might cross paths again."

"Yeah, that'd be nice... on multiple counts. Where I am, inside, I don't get to talk about this sort of stuff. It's kinda lonely."

Teeth nodded. "I can relate. And even if you could share it, well, you never quite remember yourself when you're back inside, so it never feels real, or like—"

"Or like taking a photo of the Grand Canyon," The Faceless said. "You're just never gonna do it justice."

Teeth took The Faceless's hand in her talons and smiled. "I hope we get to sit together again soon, friend."

The Faceless smiled many shifting overlapping smiles. "I'd like that," she said.

Samantha rolled her eyes, exasperated at herself. "You can tell I don't get out much. How do you like to be addressed, sister?"

The Faceless smiled, and reached up to pull away her face. As she did, a scintillating light filled her eyes and she was gone.

Carla

Carla lay on the roof, enjoying the smells of the late October air. There was the smoke of burn piles and fireplaces, and under it all, the sweet decaying scent of autumn leaves and grasses. The breeze was light and it tickled the tip of her nose as she stared up to the night sky.

The moon was huge and bright. It looked like the moon in movies when you lay adrift in a life raft, or marooned on a desert island. Below her, in the house, she could hear Mom and Dad having a tense conversation. They had asked her to go to her room so they could talk, but what they really meant was 'please leave so we can stare at each other silently then both start crying for no reason'.

Adults were weird.

She reached her hand up to the moon. The moon wasn't weird. The moon was awesome. A giant ball of talc whizzing around the planet, making the ocean move. So close you could almost touch it, but too far away to visit. Carla liked that image. After all, the moon was friendlier than the sun. You could stare at it without going blind, and you couldn't get a 'moonburn' like you could get a sunburn. Plus, there was the way the features of the moon subtly changed night after night.

Carla had never registered the whole 'face of the moon' thing until a few years ago, and was terrified of it at first. The night it clicked, the features of the moon looked horrifying, like someone screaming out in pain. It frightened Carla. She wanted the moon to stop hurting. Even Coo Coo hid from the moon, not wanting to look up at its twisted visage. Carla did the only thing she could think of and sang to the moon, trying not to look at it, but hoping she could make it feel better.

Carla laughed at herself. She was such a silly kid back then. She was nine now and knew better. Still, she was fond of the moon, even if it was just a reflective rock in the sky.

She held her hand up toward the sky, and saw that no matter how wide she spread her fingers, she couldn't eclipse the moon with her hand.

So, she made her hand into the silhouette of a bunny.

Coo Coo, the skull-ghost-thing, lay on her chest, and let out an appreciative coo, clapping lightly.

"Little Bunny Foo Foo, was hopping through the forest, when all of a sudden he met a big bad wolf!" she said, holding her left hand up in a dog-headed silhouette.

Coo Coo gasped.

"Oh no, don't eat me, Mr Wolf. I was just going down to the briar patch."

"Oh, me too," the wolf said, in Carla's most menacing big-bad-wolf voice.

"But if you go there, you will eat me and my sister, and my mom."

"No," said the wolf, "I want to get away from the hunter. We can both hide in the briars, and once the hunter leaves we can follow him to his house and steal his magic beans."

Carla kept Coo Coo entranced with her story of giants and teapots and talking animals. As she played out the adventures of Mr Wolf and Mr Bunny, her shadow puppets becoming more and more detailed until Carla became conscious of the shadows in her hands. She sat up, panic stricken. Twisting her fingers into the shapes of the different characters, her hands had become long and tendrilled, with too many fingers and way too many joints. Along her knuckles were all manner of knotted fleshy growths shaped like pigs and wolves and trees and small houses.

She laid back, stiff as a corpse. This wasn't happening. She reached up and wiggled her fingers against the moon and watched the features of her mashed-up fairytale twist and bend against the sky. She started to cry. This wasn't happening. She stared past the twisted silhouettes of her hands and up to the moon and wailed.

Then the moon blinked.

Carla watched, dumbstruck as the moon came low, filling the entirety of the sky. She saw the long, dark finger, the size of a skyscraper, reach out and gently tap her hands. She saw the twisted bits of story crumble away like old plaster, revealing the hands of a nine-year-old girl within.

"Tha- tha-thank you, Mr Moon."

The finger patted her on the head, and Carla heard a gentle "Shhh...." With that, the moon and all the night sky around it stood up and seemed to slide away over the horizon. Behind it, the late October sky looking very different, with a pale sliver of light barely visible behind a thin cover of clouds.

She looked around, but Coo Coo was nowhere to be found. Wimp.

In the distance, she could hear her mom and dad calling for her, sounding somewhere between scared and annoyed. Carla wanted to slip down and sneak back into her room, so it would look like she had been in bed all along, but she could hardly move. She was shaking badly, though she couldn't understand why.

As she held herself, trying the stop the rattling of her teeth, she felt a warm blanket wrap around her as her dad settled in by her side. She was suddenly aware of her mom down below in the yard, looking up at her with a sad, apologetic face.

"I guess you heard, huh kiddo?" her dad whispered, sounding as sad as her mom looked. "You know, me and your mamma love you very much. You know that, Right? Nothing can change that. Ever."

He was talking about grown up stuff again, and about Mom and Dad not living together. Carla's gaze locked on Samantha, and as she looked up at her little girl, Samantha began to weep. At that moment, Carla had never felt more alone. It was like a gulf had suddenly opened up between her and the people that had raised her. Carla had just touched the moon, and there was no way she would ever be able to explain that to these people.

They would never understand.

Parent-Teacher

Samantha sat at the desk and felt like a giant. Parent-Teacher conferences were a joke schools played on parents, where teachers got to gloat over the fact that your kid was exactly like you at their age, just like your parents threatened they would be.

The first part of the joke, of course, is that they always seemed to be on Thursday nights. Parents file into a room with the same setup every time; full sized adults, trying to fit their Middle-American asses into desk chairs sized for twelve-year-olds. The teachers smile at the ridiculous scene, and then proceed to talk about what the students are working on, and how wonderful the class generally is. Every line accompanied by an unspoken footnote, that implied footnote being 'except for your kid'.

Samantha didn't need the preliminary pageantry. She knew why she was there. As all the other parents filed out, she stayed behind, legs sprawled out awkwardly from beneath the miniature desk.

Mrs Hoskins, Carla's teacher, looked at her with a smirk.

"Did you have a question for me? Maybe one you didn't want to ask in front of the other parents, perhaps?"

"Not at all," Samantha retorted, "I just wanted the room to clear out before I embarrassed myself getting out from under this desk."

"Ah, yes, they can be difficult. The desks, that is. Once you get out of school you lose practice. You're Carla's mom, yes? Hmm. She clearly takes after her father."

Mrs Hoskins stepped around her desk and took her seat with a practiced dramatic exaggeration.

Samantha blinked, six eyes making a quick study of the woman. She saw a little girl encased in an armor of twisted steel and sitting on a throne of broken concrete.

Samantha half expected this. Carla's teacher wasn't just a carrier of The City. She was a transmission vector.

"At least she knows her father. How is yours?"

Mrs Hoskins smiled tightly, nostrils flaring.

Samantha gracefully extracted herself from the student desk and stood facing the woman, her shoulders square and elbows slight out-turned.

"But, I think you have more to say to me than I do to you, Mrs Hoskins."

"MIS-uhs JOHN-son," Hoskins said, rolling her eyes. "Your daughter is a very intelligent child. She excels at math, her reading is well beyond her grade level, and her skills in art and music class speak to a real talent for expression. Yes. She expresses herself constantly. You can't get her to stop expressing herself. You might even go so far as to say that she is insubordinate and disruptive. She doesn't socialize well, has no friends, and insists on going off on politically-themed rants during social studies class. It suggests that she is being highly indoctrinated at home. It raises concerns, you understand? I have spoken with the principal, and he suggests that maybe a third party should come in and assess your child, and look at her home environment to find the root of her behavioral issues."

Samantha waited a moment for her temper to pass, and smiled a broad, predatory smile.

"You know, it's uncanny, because I was having that exact line of thought. In fact, I was even discussing with the District Superintendent bringing in a third party to thoroughly examine the root of my daughter's issues. Because it's funny, it's almost like somebody is making a target of her at school, making her feel threatened. Belittling her. Trying to make an example out of her in front of other children, and even encouraging them to belittle her for her intelligence. I don't know, pushing a kid into a corner like that might cause them to lash out at the source of their distress."

"Missus Johnson—"

Samantha spoke over her with a raised palm.

"—And the funny thing is, Carla has many friends, and you know what they tell me? They tell me that you've been sanctioned before by the district and the teacher's union for your behavior. Her friends also mention that you are currently on probation for using Child Division Services to threaten parents who called you out on your behavior. So let's be clear here. I know Carla is having a rough time at home right now. Her daddy and I may be separating amicably, but that doesn't fix the hurt. However, coming to school and having a teacher stand over her and explain that 'children of broken homes have few chances to succeed in life', or that she'd grow up 'morally impaired' because of her parent's difficult decisions is pretty reprehensible. I might even go so far as to use the term 'actionable'."

Mrs Hoskins smiled sweetly. "I never suggested such a thing. I simply suggested that Carla needed to learn manners, and to know her place. Clearly, I was mistaken. She does take after her mother."

"Her aunt, more like it."

Samantha set her cell phone on the desk and pulled her hand away, showing the call time at forty-two minutes and counting.

"Me, I believe actions speak louder than words, and her father, James, he's more the 'lawyer up, cowgirl' type."

Samantha closed her eyes for a moment to examine the teacher, hoping she was having the intended effect. Yes, the woman was scared now. The right kind of scared, the sort of fear that leads to positive action. Her armor was fragile. Now was the time.

Samantha turned, looking out to the dark beyond the window. "I know you got into teaching for the best reasons. You sow each season, tending another crop of minds, and feel like you are sometimes the only one that is really looking out for them. You have carved a niche, anchored into it, and try to help the ones you can. If only parents and administrators realized that sometimes you must be hard to make something sharp gentle."

Samantha turned, and as she blinked, she could see the little girl on the throne crying, though the woman's face was dismissive.

Samantha hung up the phone and slid it back into her pocket.

"I think we understand each other. I will talk to Carla about her behavior, and maybe about why you have the approach you have. I think she will understand. I suspect we shouldn't have any more problems here, will we?"

Mrs Hoskins exhaled for the first time in several minutes.

"Mrs Johnson, I prefer to be a collaborator with parents, not an antagonist."

"Me too." Samantha smiled, as much to her as to the rebar and concrete surrounding the teacher. "But I find a little antagonism can go a long way toward mutual understanding. Have a good night."

They said their goodbyes, and Samantha turned down the hall to make her way to the parking lot. There were only two cars left. As she slid into the driver's seat, she heard a rustling and someone clearing their throat. She started the car nonchalantly, and look in her rear-view mirror at the anthropoid insect folded into the back seat. Its gleaming compound eyes were like a mantis, covered in a thin rainbow sheen from the streetlight. It looked at her, expectantly.

"There's hope for her. Give her the tools to cut her own way out, and make sure she has the breathing room to do it. The City knows we are here. Keep it off of her, and I think she'll be okay."

"And if The City comes?"

"When it comes."

"Yes, Gatekeeper, when The City comes."

"I suspect Janet Marie Gravis-Hoskins is too minor an actor to attract direct attention. Deal with the emanations as they arise, and when in doubt, ask for help. The City doesn't understand cooperation. It only understands predation."

"Right. Yes. Anything else?"

Samantha was suddenly struck by the symmetry of the moment, and smiled at the gangly creature folded uncomfortably in the backseat of her tiny car. She pulled one of the gold stars off of Carla's homework and handed it to the fledgling Guardian. It gave her a puzzled smile.

"Gold star. Good work! A+! You've got this!"

It chuckled.

"Thank you, Gatekeeper."

"Thank you. You sure didn't get an easy one for your first time, did you?"

"No, but..."

The mantis-headed Guardian looked off toward the school with a sigh.

"Did she used to be your teacher?"

The creature was silent.

"Teachers make the best students, just like nurses make the worst patients. You can do this. She can do this. Let me know if I can be of further help."

The entity raised the star with a toasting gesture, then gracefully unfolded itself from the many contours of Samantha's cramped hatchback. It nodded to her again, crept its way across the parking lot, and turned down the hall toward Mrs. Hoskin's classroom.

The Wandering Friend

There was so much work to do. The City was more active than ever, and the world was filled with unrest. But after today, none of this mattered much to Samantha. She was too tired. Lurking beneath The River, and holding Hungering Things at bay was a dangerous proposition, all the worse when you are so exhausted you can barely defend yourself from your waking life.

But it was done. She and James had been separated for almost three years now, and had come out of the proceedings as better friends than while they were married. However, seeing her name signed at the bottom of that form, the one declaring her status as 'divorced', carried a finality with it that she had not expected to hit her so hard. Kay had warned her. "All breakups are hard," she'd said, "even when it's mutual. Hell, maybe especially when it's mutual, cause you don't have nobody to blame for feeling so bad."

Samantha lay atop her sheets in the same clothes she'd worn to the lawyer's office, and stared blankly at the ceiling of her darkened room. She wanted her sister. She wanted her mamma. She wanted somebody to comfort her, to stroke her head and tell her it would be okay.

This hurt more than she expected, and that was saying something. Everyone had been so supportive, and mourned the separation with them. But now, laying alone in her bed, she felt more isolated than she had in many years. She wanted a reassuring touch or kind word, but in that moment she'd have been happy to simply close her eyes and fade from existence for a while.

She wanted to reach out to Carla, to hold her close and do the same for her, but Carla had opted to go to her grandparent's house for the weekend. James' folks had been so understanding through it all. Mr Johnson had been very clear about their feelings. His eyes had been wet and bloodshot, saying,

"He may be our boy, but don't you be forgetting we love you too. Always will."

He laughed and held Samantha tight, crying on her shoulder. "Truth told," he said, "had this happened ten years ago, I'd have said we were keeping you and finally getting rid of him. But we'll be keepin' you both, you understand?"

It was probably for the best Carla was there. She was almost a teenager now, and talking to mom or dad wasn't something that was happening readily even on a good day. She needed some space to mourn.

Thoughts began to drift, and Samantha could feel herself grow drowsy. Never before had she desired anything more than to let go and be at one with her flannel sheets. She imagined laying there, looking more than sexy with her hair in a tangled knot, hanging half off the bed, drooling, and completely comatose.

Samantha had almost managed to fall asleep when her ears were filled with a familiar ringing. It was like a whisper, the sound of TV static, a temple gong, and a waterfall. It interrupted every thought.

She groaned, frustrated at the intrusion.

She watched the ceiling fall away and become a field of tall autumn grass. She was standing now, seeing stars above her, but everything was illuminated. She saw the flickering shards of rainbow light playing over her arms and across her shadow. Before it even spoke, she could feel the Ancestor standing behind her.

She laughed. She cried. So many things were said, she knew, but as the light faded to a dim autumn glow, she could remember none of it, only that the tall bearded man before her was a friend.

He too was shaking off the experience, his eyes still watering.

"I am pleased to meet you Gatekeeper, terrible of visage. Allow me to re-introduce myself. I am called The Wandering Friend. I—"

He broke off.

Samantha, The Teeth Beneath The Dark River, realized she was staring him down and tried to relax her pose.

"I'm sorry, I don't get many visitors that aren't here to cause trouble."

"That is what... I think that is why an Ancestor saw fit to broker this introduction."

Her eyes passed over the visitor, and she noted his age and odd, lanky proportions. She smiled.

"You are a child of wild places, aren't you."

"I was born in the heart of the wood, but go where I am needed."

Go where I am needed. She bristled at the turn of phrase.

"You're a Bounder, then."

"Indeed."

"You were brought here by an Ancestor. This is not a social call."

"No, Gatekeeper, terrible of visage, it is not."

Samantha braced for the answer, even as she spoke. "What news do you bring me?"

"Not for you..."

Samantha's teeth stood on point.

"...but your daughter."

The Teeth Beneath The Dark River recoiled, trying to suppress a snarl.

She wanted to be polite. They had a common cause. But she could feel every word lash out at him with lethal intent.

"She is too young! This is not the time! Go away! This is no time for teachers!"

The Wandering Friend smiled sympathetically, looking more like a weather-worn tree than a man.

She roared at him. She bellowed profanities found in no spoken language. She tore at him and lashed at him with claw and tail and fought until she was exhausted. Her frustration and remorse poured out with every strike, and every blow against him clawed at her insides. She was suddenly painfully aware of her feelings, and felt drained. She lay gasping upon the grass, her anger spent. She could feel tears welling up from deep within.

"She's already lost so much... Why you gotta do this now?"

The Wandering Friend stroked Teeth's reptilian skull and hummed gently. It was the tuneless humming of a mother rocking her baby. It was music born of comforting instinct. Samantha could feel its effect on her, even as the fears for her daughter gnawed at her.

"You don't have to do this now..."

The Wandering Friend held her close, having grown to huge proportions, and rocked The Teeth Beneath The Dark River gently in his leafy oak arms.

There was sense of security, a feeling of peace as Teeth stared up at the stars through a thick canopy of trees, as the luminous haze of The Herder passed across the sky. Then came the sudden yet subtle shift, and she sat upon a rock by the dark river, the still waters flowing silently through the reeds. Teeth sat half upon the bank, looking down at the small Bounder, a tiny stick of a man with warm eyes and a long flowing beard that draped nearly to his knees.

Her anger had been drawn from her, leaving only a heavy feeling in her chest.

The Wandering Friend let out a sigh. "I am sorry. You have assumed correctly. I have come to be the first of your daughter's teachers."

"She isn't going to be a Bounder."

"She will be whatever she determines to be, if anything. She may reject all of this and spend her life looking away. It won't be known until it comes to pass."

Samantha rested her head on her talons with a sigh. "I knew this day would come. I just wish it wasn't now."

"And that it wasn't me."

"No, not, not you in particular, but, yeah. My sister is a Bounder, and she is effectively lost to me. I'm not comfortable with the idea of my daughter being a Bounder. I keep bad things at bay. Y'all go seeking them out. You travel into the dead heart of The City. I'm... I'm her mother. Don't I get a say or..."

His sympathetic smile and furrowed brow confirmed what she already knew.

The Teeth Beneath the Dark River groaned. "The family of a candidate aren't supposed to know anything the student does not wish to share. That's the tradition, isn't it?"

"Yes, Gatekeeper."

"Then why are you here talking to me?"

"Self-preservation. You are a Gatekeeper and one renowned for her ferocity. You are not someone I wish to surprise in my comings and goings. Also, I wish to establish ground rules. I am her teacher, and as such, I must be afforded space for the lessons."

"So then, what do you need from me?"

"I need your trust, and the assurance you will not interfere. By your nature, you keep Hungering Things at bay, but you need to examine them. Some will bear my mark, and those must be permitted to invade this twist of The Manifold."

"I can't permit Hungering Things to just wander across the water and cause havoc."

"You must. If a student cannot fend off the crushing dark, then there is no way they can walk the in-between places."

Samantha stared at him, her six eyes glowing dimly. She examined the scintillating play of light across the twig-man's ancient features. He seemed familiar somehow, like the memory of a Faceless, though it seemed he no longer had a foot on the near bank, so to speak. This

Bounder had sloughed off the waking world long ago.

"I am a Gatekeeper," she proclaimed through clenched teeth.

"And her mother." The Wandering Friend nodded. "If this could have been done without saddling you with the knowledge of the trials your daughter will face, I would. But respect, and as I said before, self-preservation, guide my decision."

"Then what do you need me to do—or not do."

"I am told that she had a number of close experiences in her youth, that she may have seen and remembered glimpses of you and your sister as you really are, and may even have some memory of the grandmother that has passed. She also has a friend, an errant geist that attends to her that—"

"Coo Coo," Samantha interjected harshly. "His name is Coo Coo. They are inseparable."

"That she has such friends without being trained is a good sign. But he needs to be sent a—"

"I promised him he would never be cast out of this house. Would you force me to be a liar?"

The Wandering friend paused. "I think only of his safety. He may need to be sent on a long errand, then."

"Whatever, you can work that out with him, but he will not be turned away."

The Wandering Friend nodded respectfully. "Very well, Gatekeeper." He spoke with a measured, even cadence. "Then that being said, let us establish the ground rules of my tutelage. You will not interfere. You will not inquire. You will not actively promote, seed, or prime your daughter as a Gatekeeper. The lessons and support you have given her up to this point now must stand on their own. Those Hungering Things that have been tampered with must be permitted through, and you may not come to your daughter's aid as Gatekeeper or Mother. You will not actively promote, seed, or prime your daughter as her waking mother either."

"This is the nature of it: First the test, then the lesson. For my part, I will be ever present in your daughter's life, waking and asleep, during these initial lessons. If she is inclined to be a Bounder, then I or another like me will continue her studies. If hers is another role, then an appropriate teacher will step forward. To be clear, if she follows the path of a Gatekeeper, then you may well know her teacher, but the ground rules would still stand: you cannot interfere."

Samantha cocked her head to give the impression of a smile, noting to herself the occasional hints of a midwestern drawl in the man's voice. "You did that all in one breath?"

"Long practice," The Wandering Friend said with a wry grin, "When you are as old as I, certain things you have down rote. So, are we agreed then?"

"Of course we are. It's not like there's a choice. Not a realistic one, anyways."

"That does seem to be the case."

"Alrighty. Then, when does—"

You shall not inquire!

The words buffeted her like a gale wind. They were her words, from within her own thoughts. By agreeing, she had entered into a contract she couldn't break any more readily than she could halt the movement of the moon. Her eyes were wide with disbelief.

"I hadn't realized I'd agreed to some kind of geas."

"If so, it is your own doing, or that of an Ancestor. I make no such compulsions. But, If I am correct, you were about to ask when will this begin?"

Teeth, Samantha, nodded.

"From what I know of you, you likely suspect that it already began long ago, and now is just the beginning of the formal lessons. You would be correct. It always seems to be that personal hardship triggers the coming of the teacher. It is a clarion call. A pupil is being made ready. Now is when they must learn to swim, fly, or walk, or whatever their mode and fashion will be. Blessed are those that have never strayed from the near-shore. Peace be upon those who have."

The Hunt

Three dire canines circled the bed, their shadowy bodies sublimating in the moonlight. Their teeth glistened and dripped, and their bright eyes were white orbs set into utter darkness. There were no dreams here. The children in the beds were so heavily medicated that the hospital ward was like a tomb, with so many little bodies stored away on slabs and shelves.

Someone had called. Someone knew their song. But now, as Hunters stalked and folded through the walls of the children's rooms, there was only a faint scent of foreboding that clung to the sheets and doors of the place.

A lean, skeletal plague-hound sniffed under a bed and snarled. His ears were low and he looked to his pack-mates with curled lips and they bristled. The diseased nightmare leapt onto the bed, and sat astride the child, staring intently at the little boy's face.

The dread mastiffs stood alert as their pack-brother dissolved into the child. One watched the bed, ears perked, muscles tense. The other watched the door, its face twisted into a rippling wall of teeth and scar tissue.

Soon, an amber light began to fill the room as a membrane encased the child. He dreamed fitfully. The diseased dog saw to that. The vague scents in the room sharpened. There was a scent of rot, of gasoline, and of seminal fluids. Then came the strong musk of The City. The dog at the bed loosed a panicked howl, and through the wall, a flowing canine form joined them. Baskerville too smelled the sick-sweet fumes and leapt upon the bed. She shoved her head through the membrane and pulling at the plague dog by the nape of his neck, freeing him from the mind of the child.

The rotting canine shook himself and shuddered. He reeked of depravity, but it had been worth it—they had their trail.

The beasts sniffed at him, snarling, hair bristling, whipping themselves into a frenzy, their pale eyes glowing malevolently.

Baskerville lunged toward the sleeping child's throat, rending at the fading membrane and tearing open a space through him. The other Hunters lunged through the gap, enlivened by the pursuit of prey.

As her last cohort passed, she released her hold, and the membrane around the forced dream faded.

The child reminded her of the boy that had spawned her. He had been so terrified of her, though she never understood why. He would look with dread into shadows and dark corners, and that is where she would find herself. She would watch him from the bushes, the heating vents, or the cracked closet door. He would look in her direction and blanch, only to quickly look away and sing loudly to shake off his fear. In those early days, he had such a wild imagination, and her form shifted many times before he gave her a name. But sometime before he started school, something changed. Something familiar terrified him more than she ever did, and her presence was practically forgotten.

She would lay beneath his bed listening to him sleep, watching the familiar feet that came in and out of the room during the night. The boy never stirred, trying to play dead while familiar hands went places they shouldn't. That is when she first smelled the musty scent-sound of something from outside. She didn't know what it was at the time, but it was danger, and she knew then that she had to scare the boy away from the life he knew. If she could drive him to safety, try to herd him away from here, he might be okay. They both might be okay.

Years went by, and still the familiar feet came and went, though not as often as before. Now, the boy slept fitfully. He lashed out at others. She was his only companion, though he never knew it. As he sketched in his journals, she could smell the musk on him and hear things circling him in the night. As he twisted and writhed in fitful dreams, she could smell that familiar, awful musk approach, and hear the grating groans and screeches of the nearing darkness. She bit and gnawed at him as he slept, hoping that if he waked, they could not reach him. She would torment him, do whatever she needed to do to wake the boy, and he would sit up in bed, drenched in sweat, doing everything he could to stifle his screams.

Then one day, the boy finally escaped his circling tormentors.

She slept beneath his body as it swung from the yew tree. It was two days before the familiar feet found him. Then there were more people than she had ever seen. There was a blur of activity and noise, and of flowing tears. Then, as quickly as it had started, it was over. They lowered the boy's body to a stretcher and took him away.

She expected that to be the final moment of her existence, watching the ambulance drive off in the pink glow of sunset. But it wasn't.

As night fell, for once, she felt cold. It was darker than she ever recalled it being. Her senses were muted, and she had only the vaguest sense of who she was and what she was doing. She was anxious. Her vision was dark, and all around her, colors slipped into darkening gray tones. She was frightened. Sounds were muffled and distant. Her breathing felt labored. If she was breathing at all. Yes, of course she was breathing. A scent! There was a scent!

She blindly charged after it, an instinctual desperation driving out all other thought. The smell grew stronger and sweeter as she ran. She yelped and barked as she barreled headlong into the darkness, nipping and biting at sustenance she could barely sense.

There was nothing left of her. There was only hunger and pursuit.

She had no idea how long this lasted, but she remembered the sudden sensation of falling upwards, and the prismatic spray of color that overwhelmed her. There was a flash of a horrible face with six lidless eyes, and then a sudden shift inward. Under the horrible gaze of the terrible visage, her memories buffeted her like a gale. She saw her life from before with a new intensity. There were emotional reactions to her memories. She didn't know what they were. Anger? Love? Dread? It was overwhelming.

For the first time ever, she thought of her boy, and joy and sorrow drew from her a howl. The sound was that of an avalanche played on an oboe. There were no words for these alien emotions. Only a mournful roar of profound loss.

Then, she heard an echo. It was a baying, guttural howl in the distance that mirrored her feelings. Then another, this one higher pitched yet as somber and plaintive as her call. More voices joined them, and the mournful chorus turned celebratory, even aggressive.

She snapped away from her recollection. In the distance, she heard the staccato 'laugh' of the plague-dog. The quarry was spotted. It was an emanation of The City. The pursuit was on. Tonight they would feed!

She gently nuzzled the sleeping boy's face, then let out an excited howl of her own as she leapt through-and-past the boy to join the hunt.

The Wall

"It stirs" was all the warning I got.

When I showed up, a small group was already milling about. Some of the men were clean-shaven, wearing elegant suits under their long, dark coats. Some looked like they had wandered out from under a bridge, with scraggy, mangy hair and matted beards. A couple looked like they were not from around here at all. They had tangled braids, broken faces, and bare, scar-torn chests, looking like they had stepped off the pages of a Viking or Pictish history.

Most of us knew each other, and introductions were made as stragglers wandered out of the shadows and gathered on the front lawn of the small, run-down home.

We spoke in hushed tones, hoping to preserve the evening's stillness. We smoked our cigarettes, or checked the time on our cellphones, shared stories and chuckled among ourselves, looking more in character as the gaggle standing outside a pub than a darkened sub-sub-urban house.

It was one of those little wedges of land the city forgot about as roads were straightened, land was bought and sold, and freeways were built. 'Mixed use, industrial-residential' is the term, I think. Cops didn't come here. Nobody did, except for the 9-5 welders and repairmen in their low rent shops.

The small house was one of only five left in this forgotten sliver of the American Dream that wasn't boarded up and overgrown. I didn't know the boy inside, but I knew his teacher and what might happen if we did not heed the call for assistance.

"It's almost three," one of the fellows said in a thick German accent as he stamped out his cigarette and put his phone away. "I am thinking we stand now."

There were nods of agreement and the gaggle fell into a line across the front of the home, each man standing shoulder to shoulder with his peers. The distant thrumming of some piece of heavy machinery became our war drum. Breaths became short and even. We breathed as one, and each could feel the predatory intensity of the man on either side of them.

When the creature came, it was as I expected it would be; a tangled mass of forms, each suggesting horrible violence, with mouths and eyes folding and unfolding between reaching, grasping appendages. It was a sloppy, incongruous ball of nightmares born from the shadows of some past trauma, now made flesh. It needed a meal, or a host. It would get neither. We stood fast before the slathering thing, our feet anchored to the very core of the earth itself. We began to speak in a slow, low tone.

"One Man. One Wall."

It was a challenge so old even cavemen would had understood it. "Hrahh!" we all exhaled as one through broad smiles, our teeth glistening.

Hrahh.

Each forceful breath was a threat, a promise to the twisting emanation before us.

Hrahh.

Hrahh.

We exhaled in time to the idle drumming of distant machinery.

The creature paused but for a moment. The eyes within eyes seemed to show some small degree of intelligence, but the thing knew it could not reverse its course. It had left the safety of its chrysalis and would wither and die. That boy was the only way. The boy. Yes, we could see the decision moments before it lunged. It tore its way across the parking lot, pushing abandoned cars and ill-kept landscaping and fences out its way as it tumbled and lurched toward us with the momentum of a freight train.

Our grins broadened to the point of hurting. It was mirth, glee, and ecstatic anticipation. The thing was faster now. It wasn't going to try to fight us. It was going to go through us. As it launched itself from the street, it became airborne. It was committed to its course, and our elation was complete.

In that moment, there was no one man there for it to crush, no wall for it to break through. Instead, it faced the inevitability of a vast, gaping mouth lined with teeth, and a horrible, twisting fractal of digestive paths beyond.

The momentum of the thing bowled us to the ground, knocking us to our senses as the digestive discomfort of our meal immediately kicked in.

Some staggered away as the pain overtook them, but most of us writhed on the ground feeling the sickest we'd ever felt since, well, that last time we did this. We lay on the grass, staring into the starless sky, laughing. The endorphins barely offset our agony, and we played at further ways to add to our meal's torment, suggesting that the only cure for something that evil was something equally evil, like strawberry horchata and Jaeger, or milk and rubbing alcohol. The well-prepared among us passed around flasks of bourbon or bottles of Pepto.

I looked to the boy's teacher. He nodded with a sour grimace and dragged himself to his feet. He traced the path of the creature back toward the direction of the river, in case there was more for him to do. There was another river, one "outside," that he would also have to visit, to report that the deed was done.

The camaraderie of the moment eventually faded to quiet contemplation. We had taken it in. It was part of each of us. Now came the hard part. They say you are what you eat. We kept gambling that this wasn't true.

There is something out there, some nasty, hungry thing that wants to feed on us. I don't understand, but I don't have to. There are many willing to hold the line and eat the dark. I suspect we've been doing this forever, and we will continue to do so as long as we are able. There is no other way.

Three Doors

Carla's teacher had been quiet and contemplative as he led her through the white stuccoed buildings and abandoned plazas of the cliffside town. They had wound upward through the city, witnessing a village with all the evidence of daily traffic, now inexplicably abandoned. It was like walking through an empty movie set.

They climbed to an upper hall in a church and stopped before three louvered doors. With a motion from her teacher they opened, and Carla gasped. Where she expected to see a sweeping view of the ocean with the city winding away below, she instead saw the sea lapping at the foot-worn thresholds of the doors.

She saw what was happening and was overcome with desperation. Beyond the first door, the sea had turned gray. The water was opaque with the bloated bodies of dead sea life. Past the second door, she saw the seas receding, leaving creatures beached, slowly dying in the sun. At the third door, she watched as the waters rose. Within reach of the door sat a planter with a small bush growing from it, and in that bush were all manner of lizards and crawling things. She reached out frantically, trying to save them. Some allowed themselves to be picked up with small grunts of protest. Others bit and stung her hands as she tried to pull them into the perceived safety of the hallway. But the waters rose too fast, and looking out through the door, she cried as she watched the remaining ones drown, unable to help them.

The doors closed and she sobbed heavy, soul-crushing tears. She felt her teacher wrap his arms around her. She wailed and screamed. The hurt was overwhelming.

"I couldn't... I couldn't save them all!"

Her teacher's voice was gentle and frail.

"I know. Now you know how we feel."

Beyond the doors, a wide vista opened out on the world, with the busy cliffside town winding down to the sea below.

Bunny

Violent Crimes Against the Homeless on the Rise

Local Homeless Man Dead
Four Suspects in Custody

Homeless Advocate Found Burned to Death
Teens Face Murder Charges
Local Residents Seek Justice

"Not My Son"
Mother Urges Judge Against Leniency

Vigilantes in the Slums
"Community Safety Groups" On Rise After Vicious Attacks

She had saved the clippings. Amid all the chaos in the world, she had found the local story unfolding on page A3 each day heartening, even if it was buried behind city council minutes or the sales going on down at the local car dealership.

Karen's imaginary friends, the voices she heard when she closed her eyes, told her to remember this. They said this would be important later, when all other kindnesses in the world had been forgotten.

She held the scrapbook to her chest on the bus. She hadn't been back to Missouri since she was a little girl, but she had a map with a history of the attacks and the stories of those that had stood up and fought back. Folded into its pages was the letter she'd received on her birthday, in 1993. The instructions had been specific, and she had always taken it as her sacred duty to carry them out, even though she could never understand why.

Karen stepped off at 'The Dreamgap' park and was met by a large plaque reading 'In the memory of Walter Elder. We love you'. The park was a corner city lot, dug out and planted as a token from the city to the neighborhood affected by such brutality. Three huge elms shaded most of the park. A large tiered fountain with a broad bench nestled in the furthest corner. At its base was a small drinking fountain bearing the inscription 'Drink up, friend. This one's on me!'

She took a sip, and sighed. "Thank you, Mr Elder."

A nasal voice from behind startled her. "Bunny. It was Bunny. Nobody called him Mr Elder."

She turned to say she was sorry, only to look down into two pale blue eyes that bugged up at her from a tiny, wrinkled face.

His voice whined and wheezed as he spoke. "We Say 'Thank you Bunny' around here. Everyone loves Bunny. We miss him. But he won this for us, which is nice. Bunny is nice."

The small man stepped up onto a small peg at the side of the drinking fountain and closed his eyes before taking a drink.

"Thank you, Bunny. Thank you, my friend," he grunted as he let himself down.

"Were you a friend of Wal— er, of Bunny?"

He arched his eyebrows for a moment like he didn't understand. "No. No, but I am a friend of Bunny. My, my name is Darryl. Darryl Hoggs. Have you ever met me?"

Karen smiled nervously. "I don't think so. I'm from Springvale."

"Oh, Springvale. I've never been there. Springvale. We've met now, so you can say that you are a friend of Bunny too, okay? Would you like a Nehi?"

Darryl took her hand, and before Karen could object to the funny little man, she found herself sitting next to an older woman in tattered jeans, and had a peach flavored soda shoved into her free hand.

"Chris... This is Chris Golding. She lives here. Chris, This is my friend Karen. She is a friend of Bunny."

Chris smiled at Darryl and up to Karen. "A friend of Bunny, huh?"

Karen smiled apologetically.

"Darryl, how about you go get me one of those too, okay dear?"

Darryl smiled and toddled off toward the bodega on the corner.

"Bless him."

"I'm sorry, I didn't mean to intrude. I was just getting a drink..."

"From Bunny's fountain."

Karen smiled sheepishly.

"Darryl is a sweetheart. Bunny was the one person in the world that cared about him. Now, it's like he tries to keep Bunny alive by being like him, poor guy." Chris edged back with her shoulders and cast a doubtful glance. "Why the interest?"

"I'm just..."

"Not a reporter doing some human-interest piece, I hope. 'The Bunny Park, twenty years later'?"

A warm breeze blew past and Karen frowned to herself.

"As a little girl, I saw the stories of what happened here. It made me scared. It made me angry. But, I kept seeing this picture of a smiling face, this fellow who looked like my grandpa, who was saying folks need to take care of each other. He died about the same time as my grandpa, so the two are forever linked, I guess. Sort of like a great uncle I never met."

Chris laughed a little. "Well then, maybe you are a friend of Bunny after all. What's the book?"

Karen offered it over. "It's just a scrapbook. Things I clipped and saved as a little girl. The things that brought me here."

Chris flipped through the pages, and her eyes teared up as she scanned the headlines.

"Walter 'Bunny' Elder had always talked about a place called The Dreamgap," Chris said, sniffing and sighing as she spoke. "It was where the homeless would be safe, without overbearing need or want. It wouldn't be heaven, he would say, but it would be a way-station for those needing to stop, even for a minute, and breathe safely."

"Hah, like this one here. 'Local Homeless Man Demands Keys to Former Savings and Loan.' Newspapers had a good laugh about that. Some bum wants the keys to the bank! I told you 'junk bonds' were a bad investment. Hurr hurr hurr."

"But Bunny was just a sweet fellow that loved to talk to folks. He'd strike up a conversation with anybody. He'd struck up a conversation while standing in line for a hotdog, and it happened to be the custodian for the empty Pennington Trust building. Being the middle of winter, he asked if there was any chance they could unlock the building when it was really cold, and the custodian said he would. Lost his job for being a decent human."

"Oh, that's sad."

"Yeah, it's sad, so what did Bunny do? He convinced everyone he met to write in the guy's name on the next ballot. It was nothing political. Bunny just felt bad for the janitor losing his job for being a good person. He figured it was a way to give him a new job. That's how Bunny was."

"What happened?"

Chris, pointed to one of the headlines in the scrapbook.

Homeless Advocate Wins City Council Seat in Surprise Upset

"In fact, Mayor Bob just recently retired and lives a few blocks from here. New mayor is a little too Tiffany and Coach to want to deal with the folks sleeping rough, but at least she doesn't go out of her way to make our lives any harder."

"Oh. I'm... I'm glad."

Chris looked at Karen, with her diamond studs and styled red hair, then turned back toward the fountain with a sigh. "Bunny was a sweet man with no good sense. Folks here needed a sweet man to put a sweet face on being homeless. A little compassion and a whole lot of pity. But folks out here, we don't need pity."

Chris stood, throwing her bag over her shoulder. "We don't need pity. We need food, water and physical security. Same as anybody else."

Karen just looked up at her and nodded. "Thank you. Sorry to have troubled you."

"You didn't trouble me, Miss Karen," she said over her shoulder as she walked away. "You're a friend of Bunny."

Karen sat in her room, a strange sense of anger and guilt mingling in her chest. She never got a chance to tell Darryl 'thank you' again, and the conversation with Chris had ended so abruptly that Karen wondered if she had said or done something to offend.

She stood and went to the restroom to wash her face, but the cool, clear water did nothing to get rid of the warm, gritty feeling on her skin and hair. She took a shower, long and hot, but it did nothing to comfort her. With a flick of the wrist, she switched the temperature to cold, hoping to shock herself out of it. Even though she now felt cold and more awake, the tugging in her chest did not abate.

She pulled her wet hair into a ponytail and got dressed. It was barely midnight, but the air was still warm as the August heat only now relaxed its grip on the city. She passed a small club where angry voices harshed it out over angrier guitars and rip thrash drums. She passed the sidewalk cafe, slowly trying to close up for the night as servers worked their way around swooning lovers that hadn't gotten the hint that it was time to go. She passed the Irish Pub with its live music and frantic fiddling, even though it looked like most folks were at their stools watching professional poker on widescreen televisions.

Then she passed the little corner store and knew she had found her way back to the park. It was so very different at night. Lights up in the trees cast heavy shadows and bright beams across the ground, and the points of light showing between the leaves gave the impression of so many little candles flickering high in the canopy.

She wandered back and sat on the wide bench of the fountain, where she could take in the whole of the park. Still feeling that she had missed something important, Karen pulled the old birthday envelope from her pocket, and once again reread the words.

I don't know who you are, but if you would pay me one kindness, you would be my friend.

In 2016, there will be a park called The Dreamgap. It isn't there now. Go there at night during the warm months. Sit at the edge of the fountain until you see my friend. When the darkness comes, hold your breath. Your life will depend on it. Give him the enclosed envelope. Please. I am trusting you.

Before this afternoon, the words had always held an air of exotic mystery to them. Now, well, they had somehow lost that luster. She had taken a bus from three hours away, but why? Did she think she was going to meet a ghost, or go on some grand adventure? The doubt physically hurt, and she wondered why she had bothered coming. Was she going to show up and be the small-town college girl that saves all the homeless people? Were they going to cry out her name, thanking her for her compassion and for having blessed them with her presence?

"God, I'm so stupid..." she sighed, burying her face in her hands. Doing so, the ancient letter crinkled against her face, and reminded Karen that she wasn't here for herself. She sighed, and returned to watching empty pools of light and shadow beneath the trees.

It was well after 3:00 AM when she noticed that the lights beyond the park had dimmed. A thick fog settled in, but rather than fill the air with the diffused warm glow of the street lights, it muted them to a darker and darker gray until everything beyond the park was a crushing black. Her eyes widened. The park existed now as a tiny island in a vast, opaque nothing. She could hear things moving in the darkness. They argued. They shouted. They screamed. There were cries for help, and so many sounds of violence. With the building intensity, she knew something terrible approached.

From the shadows of the park entrance came a terrified panting, and she saw Darryl running toward the fountain. Her heart shot into her throat. Behind him, four young men emerged from the darkness.

They were pale, with sharp features and mocking sneers. They stalked after their prey, weaving between the pools of light in polo shirts, carrying golf clubs. They laughed and grinned among each other, all the while herding Darryl toward the solitude of the park. They moved like cats, or sharks preparing to frenzy. Their predatory smiles twisted their faces into dark, malicious caricatures.

She looked on in terror as they weaved between the trees, herding him toward the back corner where she was. They hadn't noticed her yet, but she saw the terror in Darryl's eyes and could feel it growing in her own chest. She seized, locked into inaction as every muscle of her body seemed intent on pulling at the same time. Unable to act, she watched twisted forms manifest behind the boys. Their faces were vicious and gleeful. Their sickly yellow eyes were focused on Darryl, and their smiles were echoed in the quickening pace of the young men bearing down on their quarry. She wanted to shout, but a sudden cold grasp on her arms made her inhale sharply. The words of the letter flooded her mind as she was pulled backward into the churning waters of the fountain.

In the gray dim of the water, Karen saw faces. Horrible faces like the ones she had seen hovering over the attackers. They clawed at her, kicking and beating as they crawled over her and each other. Their shrieking terror was contagious, and with each boot or fist she felt the same mania grow in herself. Yet, part of her could see the actions that lead to each blow and saw down the lines of consequence, each act an attempt to escape predation. She looked up, and doing so, her eyes caught a gaping mouth of crumbling asphalt and twisted rebar. She felt the driving pulse of each action pushing the next one, all the while herding the terrified forms closer to the edge of the hungry void. She turned around to find the source of the things clawing over her, but when she looked, there was nothing there to escape. Only empty shadow. Still they came, wave after screeching wave, kicking and screaming.

She rooted her feet into the crumbling pavement. It reminded her of standing on the beach, playing in the surf. You braced against the waves, then a tall one would come, and you would either try to float over it and risk being swept away, or you let it pass over and around you. You could feel the change of pressure, and the pushing and pulling, but when the wave passed, your feet were still dug into the sand, and the sea lay stretched out all around you.

Still, the faces and hands swept over her, dragging at her, pulling her down, and her fear turned to anger. There was a muffled scream. It was Darryl. She needed to breathe. No, not Darryl. This had to stop. Bunny said he'd be safe here. He believed in Bunny. This had to stop. He's Bunny's friend. Stop. He's my friend!

STOP!

Chip watched it crawl out of the fountain. The others were too caught up in the moment. They'd found the little retard at the bus stop on 86th, after Chad gave them all a look that said 'Follow my lead'. They were just gonna mess with him, but something came over them and when the retard started trying to back away, this feeling, this need to chase him down and ruin him, grew overwhelming.

The last few minutes had been a euphoric blur, tension building as they closed in on the godforsaken little fuck. It was like the slow build of an orgasm, but now, at the moment of climax, Chip had no desire but to escape. He tried to shout, but found he had no voice, and when he tried to turn and look away, he found every muscle betrayed him.

The thing that rose from the fountain was tall and pale, with long, thick ropes of wet black hair obscuring huge white eyes. It lurched forward and let out a wet, gurgling howl. The things lips curled back, revealing row upon row of glistening needle-like teeth. Chip fell backward, stunned at the sight. Then, the others saw it and turned pale. Chad kept kicking at the tard before he saw the others staring past him. He turned on his heel to the drowned horror lurching toward them. The sound he made was somewhere between a laugh and a snarl as he charged the monster, raising his golf club like an axe. He brought the shaft down in a wide arc, but the monster lunged toward his throat with long, glistening fingers. He tried to strike at it, but before he could so much as drop his club, the creature had grabbed his shoulders and kicked with both feet, bringing all its weight down on his knees, forcing them backward.

There was a terrible pop of bursting cartilage and broken bone, and Chad let out an unearthly scream.

The euphoria that had fueled them blinked away. There was no more sense of safety in their actions. They were exposed. Chip grabbed Chad's shoulders, pulling him away from the monster that stood over him. He turned, looking for the safety of darkness, but saw only the brilliant flare of red and blue light, cops silhouetted in the yellow glow of street lights, barking orders to get on the ground or else.

Chris later said it was fortunate that they were too stupid to comply.

Locals didn't talk about that night. It was just another bad memory in a string of bad memories, but it seemed to have been the last attack anywhere near The Dreamgap.

The two women sat on the bench, contemplating the fountain. Darryl came up and said hello, he wanted to tell them about the new squirrels he'd met. There were new squirrels this year, you see. They met him. He was walking better too, but that night still left him in rough shape. And thank you for the letter. Bunny is my friend. You are too.

Then, Darryl saw someone new to the park. They were getting a drink, and he needed to go find out if they were a friend of Bunny.

Karen smiled after him, and Chris watched her friend with a deep appreciation. The sun would set soon, and her heart swelled. She was no longer alone holding vigil against the crushing dark.

Citymouth

The cars slowed, forcing him to a stop. His stomach leapt.

Mike didn't know this part of town. Honestly, he didn't know what turn he'd made that took him from his familiar commute into this industrial-area-from-hell. Cul-de-sacs, roads passing through parking lots, one-way streets, and chained driveways all dead-set on him not getting home. It was after 7:00 PM, but the asphalt still radiated the summer heat, and the humidity was miserable.

The GPS in his car had started spouting nonsensical directions twenty minutes ago and he could not get it to shut up.

"In five feet, turn left."

Yeah, right into the wall of a building.

"Proceed forward."

Oh, sure, right through the three-way intersection and into a drainage pond.

Arguing with the failing device, he hadn't noticed the cars following him.

Mike hadn't seen another car on the road in the last half hour, and now he was being forced to stop by two army-green Landcruisers. As he slowed, he got a brief glance of the vehicle's occupants, with their paramilitary outfitter clothing and shaved heads, and his heart raced.

They were getting out of the cars. They were pulling guns and training them on him. They were yelling at him, approaching the passenger door of his car. The barking staccato of their shouts made him think of mastiffs. They had faces like mastiffs, with flapping jowls and eyes that burned like hate.

He reached for his gun. Mike had never owned a gun. Never even held one, but he had one now and did not question this. He crawled out the driver's side window, firing haphazardly at the dog-faced security guards, who now took cover, still barking commands and accusations and epithets. The air filled with barked shouts from every direction. His ears hurt. His heart hurt.

His eyes locked onto a figure fleeing one of the vehicles. Mike's pain stopped. Even as he raised his hand to fire, a thought in the back of his mind screamed against it. He chased after this other man, firing repeatedly, missing as the guy fell and rolled to the ground. Mike couldn't make out a face, and the man's form shifted and morphed as he tried to escape Mike's fevered volley.

Mike ran to the man, firing on him as he lay prone on the ground, consumed by panic. All the while, he could hear a noise growing, a thought screaming in the back of his mind. "STOP!" he cried out to himself, "Why would I do this? Oh shit, why did I shoot him? Why?"

His panic consumed him. He knew he would be pursued. He knew he would be killed. He knew his family would never know what happened to him. These things were unquestionable. He saw the body of the man he had just killed. It was creaking and swelling. The body tore near the wounds, releasing a blue-white smoke. The smell reminded Mike of antiseptics, of hospitals, of that time after the accident...

Mike ran. His muscles strained and his lungs hurt. The character of the streets and warehouses had changed. Fences and steel siding were twisted and decayed and the skeletal fingers of rebar jutted out of broken concrete forms. But he was being pursued. There were no thoughts, only a terror-stricken dash down any open path he could see.

He struggled to breathe. His lungs pushed and pushed for air, but he felt faint. Muscles already taxed with oxygen starvation gave way, spilling Mike to the ground. The dense antiseptic cloud was upon him, filling his lungs and wrapping around him, squeezing him.

He cried as a shudder of exhaustion passed through the whole of his being. Every cell of his body knew only surrender. Then something changed. The panic passed.

He felt there was another with him on the broken concrete. He surrendered to the feeling of terror and in its passing there came a sense of warmth and sudden safety.

He clung to the misty form around him, wailing. For once, he heard a sound that wasn't the pounding of his heart. It was a voice, a soothing voice that reminded him of his aunt when he was little. A gentle hand stroked his neck and shoulders. A quiet southern accent whispered softly as it rocked him. "Shhh child, it's okay... you okay... jus' a bad dream child... shhh..."

Mike's sobbing passed. He gave in to the voice and the gentle rocking. Overcome by peace and exhaustion, his form faded from view.

In the quiet stillness of the ruined street, the dense cloud slowly coalesced into a tall nightmarish form. It was a slender, luminous thing with many bat-like faces and huge, leathery wings like something a child lost in the woods might have dreamt of, with many long arms and slender, padded fingers. It looked in the direction Mike had been running. There, the pavement and remains of buildings twisted and grew together into a great maw. The detritus of the street narrowed and pointed inward, drawing prey inexorably forward and preventing escape.

The Monitor looked on as the great mouth slowly closed, growling at the loss of its prey. A twinge of pride flared in its heart, and the Monitor permitted itself a moment of self-satisfaction, raising its many hands toward the retreating hellmouth, saluting with one finger of each hand before it too faded back to The Manifold.

Arthur

Carla lay perched at the edge of the man's awareness, contemplating how she would describe her relationship to him if he asked. Fairy Godmother? Anonymous Benefactor? Thing under the bed? It wasn't the first time she wondered about it. She hadn't been raised to believe in things that go bump in the night, or so she told herself, yet here she was, lurking at the periphery of co-linear space.

When she was about sixteen, she had tried to tell her parents about her 'night job', hinting at stepping outside sensed reality into the multiform multitude of interwoven time/space overlays. Her Dad just smiled and said she was very creative, just like her mom. She tried talking with mom's boyfriend, the former 'sure, I'll smoke that' hippy. Surprisingly, he started going on about spiritual warfare and that he would like her to pray with him. She conceded.

The prayer was one about avoiding the dangers of drugs and rock music. She hid behind her hair, hoping he didn't catch her smirking.

Mom, on the other hand, gave her a sad expression and changed the subject.

Spiritual warfare. You could probably call it that, if you wanted to muddy the issue. Nothing spiritual or martial about it. More like being a beat cop in a 20's film. You walked the neighborhood. You knew every brick and crack on your street, and you knew everybody on your watch. It wasn't that different. Except that part about it not being a street, and instead of being a cop you were a many-faced, protean beast of your own imagining. But beyond that, yeah, it was fairly similar.

But tonight was unusual. There was no passing silently through the rooms reflected in mirrors or across the cluttered shadows of trees.

If anything, tonight was a stakeout.

She didn't know the man sitting at his kitchen table, staring despondently at unpaid bills and obituaries, but she called him Arthur. He struck her as an 'Arthur'. Middle class, middle aged, Middle America. Probably at the top of his career until recently. Then there was a tragedy, followed by the usual string of compounding circumstances and losses. His life spiraling down the toilet, unable to see options or ask for help. He had no friends to speak of, and no family to speak to.

Soon, he would see only one way out, whatever it was, and make a decision that would end all of this. Maybe he would get a call from an old friend. Maybe he would see an ad for a trip to France. There was the possibility he might hurt himself or others. These were all very real possibilities, though she was holding out for the vacation. It helps to reinvent yourself from time to time.

Tragic as it all was, her concern was that no matter what, he did not become food for one of *Them*. The last thing she wanted was to see another empty husk, walking around like it was alive. The first one she could not save scared her from this work for nearly a year. It took an old friend and former teacher to talk her back to tending the in-between places. She had lost others. Statistically, it was unavoidable. There were far more unspeakable horrors in the world than Bounders, but that didn't mean every one she missed wasn't a punch to her heart.

She waited patiently, watching the flowing folding of events blend and merge, looking for movement in the timeless edges where everything that ever happened is happening all at once. This is where They, the Hungering Ones, swoop in from. She wrapped herself around this night in Arthur's life, sheathing it in brilliant colors and patterns, that They may pass it up.

The clock in Arthur's kitchen hung at 3:12 AM when the first Hungering Ones flocked and swarmed through the co-sensual now. They passed in and out of time, lunging into dreams and delusions, feeding on desperation. They were a nuisance for most people, but for someone in Arthur's state, even the little ones could be too much. A swarm like that could easily establish a

colony, and that would make life complicated for everybody.

Time drifted on. The many Arthurs-that-
could-be began to differentiate, like colored
swirls of paint in water. She was pleased
that he was so numb, so utterly destroyed
inside that the swirling potential that
Arthur might kill himself tonight grew
thinner and thinner. Though she knew that
she could not interfere, it wasn't something
she wanted to see again. Sadly, the streak of
time where he simply laid down and never
got up again became a stronger color. It
became a thick rope of swirling potentials
that would mean he was forever easy prey
and would need to be contained.

If Arthur had to be contained, it would be
her job to do it. She was filled with dread
and resentment that she would be tied to
this one faltering soul until he finally died,
and the echoes of his life finally faded from
all memory. That would take a while. She
didn't know who Arthur was, but his life
had greatly affected many others. So many
threads traced back to him. She wondered if
he even knew this. He must not have. If
Arthur could see what she saw, well, she

wouldn't have to be hovering in the shadows filling every corner of his kitchen.

A gray-green fog, an emanation of The City, drifted slowly by. Passing over her and around her, it felt like twigs, or fingers, running down her body and sent a revulsed shudder through her. You could not lash out at a fog, lest it learn what you guarded. If it did, it would linger, drawing the attention of more persistent and hungrier entities. Finding no meal, the fog passed as slowly as it had approached, tasting at the minds it encountered.

She eyed the cloud cautiously. It had found minds nearby dreaming of elections and wars and work, and it slowed to graze. Every fraction of time made her more nervous that a large, looming predator may come and overpower her to get to Arthur. She realized then that her own fears made her a liability to the poor man sitting at his table. For him, it was nearly 5:00 AM. He must be exhausted. Once he fell asleep, he would be someone else's problem.

She infused herself into the ribbons of color and potential, flattening the geometry of the kitchen so she could see every Now simultaneously. She wanted to nudge him. To frighten him. She would deny it, but she even wanted to hug him, and let him know that he wasn't alone.

She loved her job, but sometimes it sucked. There were mornings when she awoke with the awful feeling that it was all in vain, and no good could come of it. People like Arthur needed fellowship and a reassuring ear. It didn't matter to them that giant shadow monsters guarded them against trans-dimensional psychic parasites with a taste for human brains. Folks needed love, patience, and understanding, damnit, not Casper-The-Friendly armed with a bazooka.

She watched with dismay as the gray swirl of potential spread. This would be her life now, night after night, until she was finally released from guarding Arthur and his memory. If she made a habit of having a fixed appearance, it would have been twisted into a many-mouthed grimace.

So focused on how Arthur's degradation affected her, she almost missed the tiny yellow streaks of potential blending into this night's possible outcomes. In fact, it was Arthur rising from the table, a searching look on his face that had startled her to awareness. She shifted her point of view as Arthur opened the front door and a strong burst of yellow streaked into the gray potentials of the evening. On the porch paced a thin mutt, a labrashnitzlepoo retriever from the look of it. It looked up at Arthur with large sad eyes, and sat, shivering.

She could see Arthur was moved, but it was not enough. While she could not interfere with him, the dog was fair game! As subtly as she could, she shaped an icy breeze to sweep over the dog, quickening its shiver. That the breeze might blow in on Arthur, chilling him, causing his heart to break for this poor dog was totally not a consideration going on in her head at the time. Absolutely not. Perish the thought.

Arthur shuddered and reached over to the coat rack, grabbing his old work jacket to wrap around the dog and carried it over to the couch. He left the room to get water for it, and lacking any dog food, brought the half-eaten sandwich from the table. The dog ate the sandwich in small bites and licked Arthur's face. Carla could see his heart stirring. She could see the thick ropey swirls of yellow extending from this night, turning into luminous cords of inter-connected light.

Arthur fell asleep with the dog on the couch, small tears oozing down his face. He was no longer a low spot in the stream, an eddy where bad things could gather.

Carla smiled inwardly at the scene for some time, until a familiar panic hit her. She could feel herself waking, and did her best to brace for impact. She repeated to herself the important parts of what happened, that things she might need to cogitate upon while waking. Details like, how many Hungerings came? When did they strike? Were there any other interested entities? Did everything turn out okay?

She repeated the narrative to herself over and over, but then she was hit by a sudden doubt. Where did that dog come from? She had watched all the external factors that could have influenced Arthur. Nowhere in those had there been an animal involved. Was she remembering the wrong things?

But it was too late. She lay in bed, staring at the oh-so-persistent alarm clock, feeling like she had just been robbed of some important discovery.

Transcript

Harrington Professional Transcription Services
Order# 34Z783 Doc# MT000235

<< BEGIN AUDIO >>

[T] Alright, Mr J—, what would you like to talk about this week?

[J] What do I wanna talk about? I'm done talking. You the one that hasn't been listening, and I can't do no thinking for you.

[T] Have you been staying up on your new med plan?

[J] I have.

[T] Have you noticed any changes?

[J] <laughing — Sarcasm, fade exasperation>

Doc, I notice lots of changes. I notice more people dyin'. I notice more people angry, scared, and blamin' each other. All God's children seem to have one goal, and that's to tear each other to ragged shreds. I mean literal bloody rags. Kill. Maim. Burn. That sort of thing. It's an intensity, a desperation. If someone tryin' to climb the wall, fuck him, pull him down so you can get over it. Drowning sailors clawing over each other to get to the surface will all drown together. Yeah, the new dosage is great. I see the shit, but I can't smell it.

But you know what I can smell? I can smell the fresh bread from the bakery when I get on the bus after I leave here. I was smellin' flowers blooming in the park, and clothes drying on the line. I can smell children goin' to school and learning to play together, drawing with crayons and chasin' bugs. I can smell mommies and daddies getting down as soon as the kids are away, and maybe making a few more.

I can smell the fresh breeze sweeping over the graveyard. So yeah, yeah, I like these new drugs you got me on. They're good.

[T] And what graveyard is that?

[J] Metaphorical graveyard. The broken buildings and broken bodies, and broken spirits. I can see the skeletons, but I can smell the flowers growing up through the bones.

[T] Would this graveyard be the same as this 'city' you mentioned before?

[J] I love how you think you know what I'm talking about. You don't know enough to ask the question you wanna ask, the one you need be asking, then take whatever answer you get and try to backfill what you don't know. Damnedest logical fallacy I ever seen. There's probably a Latin name for it too."

[T] What should I be asking?

[J] Should be asking why your children's children's children are eating each other and cuss your ever living. Should be asking how you kill the parasite without hurting the host. Should be asking how we get sick from stuff that grows in our own guts.

[T] Is that what the city is? A parasitic infection?

[J] Ah, there you go again...

[T] Alright, let's change the—

[J] Aw no, you getting close. But if I explain it, you file it away in some list of 'crazy shit patients say' and trot it out when you're sitting at a hotel bar trying to get a blowjob from the waitress. No, you gotta find it yourself. You have to feel it at your throat, know how truly terrible it is. Then, well, this conversation would be a lot different. You never talk to nobody the same way after that.

[T] You mean I wouldn't assume that they're crazy or need to be fixed?

[J] Yes. No. No, you know what, it's that you think you know how the brain works. You think you know how this lump of sugar and fat connects to the cosmos. It's just a little computer—just a little robot behind your eyes going beep beep bloop beep beep.

[T] I don't think anybody that actually studies the brain thinks that any more.

[J] Yeah, but the kids do, and the lady at the clinic does. "He's got a bad CPU" I heard one say. But it ain't a bad processor, no. It's that I got more inputs than a keyboard and mouse. I was reading—I was reading an article the other day, you so smart, I was reading an article, and you know how many senses we got?

[T] In humans? I think at this point we're up to eleven that are broadly agreed on, and up to twenty-two that are still up for debate.

[J] Hooo, you are on top of things!

[T] And in other plants and animals, a whole lot more.

[J] Yeah, well, I'm just sayin that a whole lot of them ones that are still up for debate. I got. I got problems. Won't deny, but I smell things that don't have no smell, and I see shadows that things don't cast.

[T] Has your sleep improved?

[J] Since all the shit goin' on out there right now? Oh hell no. They got folks wandering around just looking to beat the fuck outta someone like me.

[T] But when you can sleep?

[J] I still hear the voices, the ones that say it'll be alright. The one's that say get up, someone's coming, run. I hear the other voices, the ones crying, the echoes of "help, is there anyone there?" I can't do nothing for them, so I just shed a little tear and keep my mouth shut.

[T] Do you really?

[J] <long pause> <laugh> No, I guess I don't then, now do I?

[T] How is the advocacy work going?

[J] Since Bunny's death, people really paying attention. They've been saying they care for a long time, but something changed. I got more people making eye contact. I got cops in the park, talkin' with ya not at ya. Everybody feel they let that boy down. He was our Jesus, and now we all carrying his cross, you know.

I swear I heard from him. I know he's gone and all, but I swear I heard from him. He said he's gonna miss Bert's chili dogs, but he sees the good that's come. He said he sees the good that's coming. We all just keep trying, reaching, ya know.

[T] Some say the ones we love never really leave us.

[J] <Laughing> He said his Granny Dee came for him. Like hell he was stickin' round to see how we clean this all up. He said it was up to us now. Course, I figure, it always was. He just was the heart, you know, or those paddles they use on TV when a doc gotta jumpstart the heart. We're the ones that keep beatin'. The City can't eat a beatin' heart.

[T] The City knows this.

[J] Yeah. <long pause> Yeah, The City knows this. But you know what too?

[T] It knows we know.

[J] <long pause> You... <long pause> I think I need to go. I done spent my hour, other people need this chair. I see you around Doc. You keep laughing.

[T] I'll see you next week Mr J—.

[J] It's B—, please, and yeah, see you next week. Maybe sooner. Bless you.

<< END AUDIO >>
<< END TRANSCRIPTION >>

A Fairytale

The geists loomed nervously. This was dangerous ground, so close to the glowing Manifold and the lumbering, shambling horrors that tended the luminous flow of dreams. It was too bright to look at, but something drove them forward. Was it hunger? Fear? They could not tell. Truth was, as they looked across the playing lights and luminous webbing that bound it all together, they weren't really sure at what point they had come into being. All they knew was that there was something terrible behind them, and that this was their only chance to survive.

A small, toad-faced thing with long, gecko-like fingers croaked to himself and gestured for the other dark wispy entities to follow. They crept along their low, shaded path until it forked, one path leading into the darkness of a great woodland. The other fork was worn smooth and descended gently toward a slow, wide river.

The toad-faced one paused, and the geists behind him grumbled among themselves. They saw his indecision and could hear his thoughts. They were not going back into darkness. There was no food in the darkness. There was food across the water. A thing was coming. We must eat. A thing is coming after us. We do not want to die! We go to the river!

Toad-face knew he had been usurped and trailed behind, always looking back to the dark of the woods. There was something comfortable about it. Familiar. He was hungry, yes, but curious. He just wanted to know... Why...

He heard hissing screams, like hot steel quenched in water. He turned to see the geists that had tried to cross the water as they were dragged down by a great monster with the skeletal head of a great reptile. The few remaining geists huddled at the shore until the water returned to a black, mirrored calm.

They packed close to the edge of the water, so tight that they blended into each other. They trembled and murmured. They prodded and goaded. Then, one reached a single shadowed tendril out over the dark river.

The surface exploded, and the same horrific creature stormed upon the shore, swallowing the geists in a single snap of its long, razor-filled mouth. Its huge talons held the banks, and the toad-faced geist watched the beast chew and swallow his former traveling companions. He stared as the beast fed, wondering why he felt no reaction to what he had just seen. What was his relation to the other geists? They had no shared history before a few minutes ago, and what history they shared was one of being snubbed for being cautious, being ostracized, and then seeing those that mocked him meet a grisly end.

The little geist couldn't tell if he felt good or bad about this.

As he contemplated his feelings, the six empty sockets in the river monster's face turned toward him and illuminated with a dim blue light. He could see a scattered prismatic sheen running along the beast's contours, and as terrible and ambiguous as the threat behind him was, this river monster could not be overlooked. All things being equal, it seemed best to accept the concrete promise of harm before him over any abstract threat that loomed behind.

He crept back into the forest, and nestled in among the rotting detritus of the forest floor. There was a light here. It was the same scintillating iridescence as The Manifold he had set eyes on before, but it was different. There was no direct source. He crawled about in the piled leaves and fallen trees, and saw how everything was cast in the same shifting ambient hues.

His hunger was strong. He shoved leaves and bark into his mouth, but they tasted foul, and he spat them out. He sniffed at the shelf fungus growing on the rotten stumps, but they smelled bitter and tasted even worse. He felt himself weakening and crawled deeper into the wood.

His head swam and he collapsed onto his back in a small clearing. Above, a bright thing shone down on him with a pale blue light like the eyes of the beast back at the river. His mind traced out the shapes of light and dark and saw something like his own face shining down on him.

Toad-face smiled, enamored with the light hanging above him. He watched as it slowly drifted across the sky, growing larger and larger, as if it were coming down to him. He reached up to touch it, but he could barely lift his arms. He sank back, and a frown formed under the moon. The geist felt himself lifted as everything went black.

The smell was delightful and overwhelming. It filled his senses and he felt his hunger consume him. He gnawed and bit and sucked and chewed at the viscera in his arms. The taste and scent made him euphoric. As his head lolled back, he saw that familiar, welcoming orb, and the black, shaggy face of the sky it was set in.

The Herder looked down at the little geist, concern furrowing its cyclopean brow. It brought its hand close to sniff and see if the little monster yet lived. The geist, in his revel, intoxicated by the light of The

Herder's eye, bit down hard and clung to the tip of the lumbering creature's nose.

The Herder shrugged, and returned to tending the slow advance of trees, rocks, and glaciers. It was so used to this fast-paced life, measured on a geologic scale, that it would have gotten bored doing anything else. It had been a long time since it had an audience, so it proceeded to go about the wild, in-between places, naming relationships between things to its new little friend.

"On..." The Herder groaned, positioning small boulders atop each other with its long, thin fingers "Supports... Anchors... Presses..."

"In... Contains... Armors... Hides..."

The geist listened, nursing at the titanic beast's flesh.

After an age of names, the geist released his bite and uttered his first words.

"Anchors nurtures me you."

The Herder smiled and lifted the geist up to its ear where he could cling to The Herder's head and see the world as it saw the world. Now the lesson changed. Things were given names and those names carried relationships. "Rock on a hill... Rolling rock on a hill... Flying rock over a hill..."

The geist clapped excitedly at the violent clatter and crashing of the massive granite boulder colliding with the darkened landscape.

The geist fed and watched the world from high above as The Herder traveled the land, gently nudging every plant and tree and stone. It moved tiny seeds that had just begun to sprout, and shaped the hills to gently change the curves of rivers. All around, little creatures scrambled to lock the world into place, while The Herder, patiently and gently eroded coastlines, shepherded mountains, and spread green tangles of vine and tree over whole empires.

The geist grew larger, older, and stronger, and the day came when The Herder lowered him to the ground and smiled.

"Anchors nurture you me. Me you."

The Herder guided the toad-faced geist to the edge of the dark water and slapped the surface. As it did, the river monster arose, teeth glistening. Toad-face had forgotten this monster and what had happened before, but as quickly as he had become afraid, the geist saw how tiny the monster was compared to The Herder. The beast was unimpressive, to say the least.

The Herder lowered its massive head to the river monster. "Shadows... need help. I... bring help."

The little one felt confused. There was pride, but there was sorrow. It could not tell whether either of these were good or bad, and so chose to simply grimace. Feelings were complicated.

The Herder set a finger on the geist's shoulder, water welting up from its giant moon-eye. "Forest home you. Listen shadows you as listen me."

And then with one silent turn, it stepped beyond the woods and vanished beyond the horizon.

The geist stifled a sigh and turned to the horrible river monster, which now seemed less like a monster and more like a bunch of dead things that had been badly bound together.

"Help you me. Show where me."

The river monster's eyes glowed, and she lifted the creature upon her back, ferrying him across the still, dark water to the glistening webs of The Manifold.

"Do you have a name?" the beast growled as they trod up from the banks and across the broken gray landscape.

"First memory... Toad Face."

"You sound reluctant."

"No, not good. Later name."

They wandered among the lights, passed over and around the phantasmagoria of the sleeping world. The geist fell in love with it. It was horrible and beautiful, an indescribable river of lights and sensations.

The feeling of stepping out the other side was a cold one, and the geist, still riding atop the river monster's back, looked out from the cliff they now stood on. In the distance grew what appeared to the geist as a black, crystalline mass. It slowly spread, sharp angles reaching, locking down everything it surrounded. Its tall spires were illuminated from within by a miasmic, sickly glow. It thrummed and vibrated with a sensation between a sound and a scent. It looked, in a word, delicious.

"Does that frighten you?" the river beast asked, noticing the little geist quivering.

"Beautiful. Eat it me. Yes."

The river monster snorted. "That is a little too big for anyone to eat. That is called The City. It wants to eat everything."

The geist shook its head. "No. Eat it me. Little bites. Many little bites. Show me, Moon-Eye. Little change big change. Yes.

Eat it me. All up. Remain only nubby bits. Mmmm!"

The geist danced and drooled upon the river monster's back and she laughed.

"Just gonna eat The City, huh?"

"Hmm, yes, eat The City. Eat The City me. Me Eat The City. Yes!"

"Alright then... Eat The City. I think I know just how you can help. But first, let's talk about your grammar, because I'm having some serious trouble with your Yoda-speak."

The Fountain

Barry had been here before. This fountain, with its peculiar seashell motif, was like nothing he had seen in his waking life, but as he ran his fingers over the sculptural details there was no denying it. The familiarity was unmistakable. He had lived many nights at this fountain.

The fountain existed in a tiny patch of ill-kempt city center, illuminated from above by some unseen source. Beyond the pool of light, the dandelion-choked bricks of the plaza faded into an opaque nothingness.

This fountain was the world.

He leaned against the fountain and folded his arms. Every other time he had been here, there had been a teacher. This is where the Black Dog taught him he could eat fear. This is where The Turtle showed him persistence and to be immovable. This is where the Luminous Grandmother told him that, no matter what, everything was going to be alright.

Now, however. He was alone, and the solitude shook him.

He couldn't account for the source, but the weight of despair was a physical hurt. He gripped the fountain, feeling the cold stonework in his hands and tried to anchor himself, but the feeling only grew more intense.

Grandmother said there would be tests if he continued down this path. He wondered if this was part of one.

As he cleaved to the fountain, he heard a rustle of wings. He turned and saw a hooded figure approach. It didn't belong here, whatever it was, but somehow the aching, crushing feeling lifted as the entity approached.

"Are you here for me?"

The thing pulled back its hood, and the young boy was surprised to see a face like his grandfather. Or was it his mother? He couldn't quite tell. The face shifted and moved fluidly from one set of features to the next.

"Yes," he said in a warm, hearty voice, "but not specifically. May I? May I have a seat?"

"Oh sure, please," Barry said, embarrassed by his own lack of manners.

"You aren't one of my teachers, are you? You are something else."

The entity smiled, if you could call it that. It was a warm expression at least, playing out across countless shifting features.

"Everyone is a teacher. That is the first lesson of a good student. The excellent student seeks to learn what kind of lesson each teacher offers. But no, I do not believe I have ever had the pleasure of your acquaintance."

Barry looked doubtful. "Why are you here, then?"

"I am... returning a favor. Think of me as a freelance Friend of Humanity. A wandering friend. You looked like you needed a friend, so I hope you will pardon the intrusion."

Barry smirked. "Naw, it's fine. I was just... waiting..."

"Oh. I thought this was your personal retreat. An anchor, if you will. If I am interrupting-"

"No, no! It's fine. It's just that every time—"

He broke off. The expression on the entity's shifting face mirrored his own.

"Aah, I think I see. This is a place of revelation for you, isn't it? But now, after all you have witnessed, after all you have experienced, you come here and find it empty."

Barry looked away.

The entity patted Barry on the knee. "I have sat where you sat. You've stepped outside many, many times, haven't you? Traveled wide roads and narrow trails that exist in the in-between. You've stood on two banks of a river and felt them moving away from each other. Stood atop a cliff as stone fell away beneath your feet, hmm? I reckon so."

Barry nodded without thinking. A question, a doubt, burned in his chest. He had never put the words to it. He had not wanted to seem disrespectful or ungrateful to the Ancestors with too many questions. But here, now, was someone or something that was like a peer. He stared intently at his feet, sculpting the words that took shape in his mouth.

"What comes after this?" he asked, hoping his words were stripped of doubt or frustration. "I feel like I've been being groomed since childhood. I close my eyes, and there is someone, umm, 'not from around here,' standing over my shoulder and showing me things I could never have imagined. I thought—I dunno, I thought there was a threshold, you know, like graduation day, a line you crossed, and suddenly, pow! Level up! Something! A higher consciousness, or some sort of sight beyond seeing. But there isn't, is there? There is only becoming. Ever becoming. What am I supposed to do with this?"

The entity looked away and let out a weary sigh. "I don't know, young man. I have been around for a long time, and I don't know what you're 'supposed' to do with this. All I know is what I chose to do with this. I too was blessed by many teachers with many names, and even more faces. That would be gift enough. But the lessons kept coming, even though I feel like they are wasted on me. I am humbled, and overwhelmed by gratitude, so I try to express it at every opportunity."

"To have teachers such as these..." Barry intoned.

"Is a great blessing, indeed," the entity replied.

They sat in silence for a long time, lost in an eternal present.

"It's just... How many of us are there? You know? I feel like I'm walking around with this terrible, awesome secret and I can't tell them. I've tried but it gets lost in the telling. It's... lonely."

The entity nodded with a kind, ever-shifting smile. "Many. Many upon many, but never enough. If you are attentive though, you will come to recognize your own. But back inside, it's not an easy thing to discuss, as you know. Some things are easier done than said."

"I—I want to help others. I don't know how, but I do. I'm just, I'm just scared to reach out, to put myself out there."

The entity smiled. "I learned long ago that it was easier to stand in defense of another than yourself. There is no lack of ways to help others, and there's surely no lack of need. But may I offer you some advice?"

"Yeah."

"One, the silence of Ancestors is not a rebuke nor an abandonment, and two, don't let anyone try to convince you that you are a holy man."

"I'm not, though."

"Good, remember that. So many seek but are quick to cling to a teacher, mistaking them for the lesson. Don't be one of them."

There was another rustling of wings.

Barry spun around and saw the Ancestor, like a great heron, standing in the fountain. He bowed his head, crying, overwhelmed by the words, "To have teachers such as these."

The heron looked to the entity and waves of colored light rippled over its body.

The entity stood with a gentle bow and raised his hood over his head, a prismatic sheen passing across his shaded face. "My pleasure. Not a worry at all. I was passing by. Just doing for another as was done for me."

The heron whistled, and there was another scintillating play of light.

The entity patted the boy on the shoulder, nodded to the Ancestor, and receded into the dark beyond the fountain.

Barry turned to the Ancestor. It looked at him warmly, waves of brilliance sublimating from its form.

Barry nodded in response to some unspoken question and looked up into the warm, glowing eyes.

"I am ready," he replied.

It was the first time ever, standing before the Ancestor, that he felt like he truly was.

Epilogue

Carla, The Face At The Darkened Window, answered the call, Coo Coo drifting along beside. She folded from one dream to the next as she followed the Hunters' howls, and began to worry as the song led her to the far banks of The Dark River.

Was something coming? Had her youngest finally passed his trials? Was another Bounder in need? Her thoughts raced over the potential crises and how to face them.

But no, it was worse than she expected. Her grand-daughter Zoe, deep in dream, played at the water's edge. She laughed and squealed, jumping in the sand, trying to touch the skeletal snout of The Teeth Beneath The Dark River, The Gatekeeper, terrible of visage.

Six glowing eyes stared disdainfully from the monster's massive crocodilian skull.

"Is this... yours?" The monster growled as it scratched at the damp sand of the river bank.

"Yes, sort of, Gatekeeper." she said, sidling along the beach, dragging her tails in the dirt.

"This child thing has crossed The Dark River. It must be dealt with. Where is her Guardian?" the beast growled, clawing the earth.

Carla looked down and smiled as she scuffed her feet in response. "She doesn't have one yet. All who have come she has rebuked and turned away."

The great Gatekeeper growled. "I think I know just the person to handle this then, Bounder, since you seem so ill equipped. Until then... take this child away from here. Now."

The Face At The Darkened Window bowed, grinning, tears seeping from her many eyes. "Why yes. Of course, oh Gatekeeper, terrible of visage. At once."

The Teeth Beneath The Dark River snarled, and the Bounder gathered up the dreaming child and led her away to the safety of The Manifold. Once she was gone, Teeth lowered herself to the water's edge and read the exaggerated letters scrawled in the sand one last time before wiping the bank clean. Words of love between mother and child scratched in the earth. Samantha had been dust many years now, and there was no talking with the dead. But then again, Teeth had never been one for following rules too closely. Being beneath the river, she never really stood on either bank, anyways.

About The Author

Clarence L Harper IV is an insufferable meddler that makes Mr Toad look like a paragon of self-discipline. When not poking stories with a stick, he is anthropomorphizing backyard wildlife and creating tangled webs of intrigue between the crows of the Southern Marches versus the Squirrel-Jay alliance of the north. You can learn more at leveritepress.com.